A Note to Readers

While Louisa and Henry Lankford and their friends are fictional, many of the events and characters in this book are not. In 1836, James Birney, a man who was strongly opposed to slavery, started printing the *Philanthropist,* a newspaper in Cincinnati. Many people were so upset by what he wrote that they tried to destroy the press. First they broke into the print shop and damaged the press. An unnamed boy who slept in the printing office (and on whom the character of Abe in this book is based) was blindfolded so that he would not see who was doing the damage.

When this didn't stop Mr. Birney from printing his paper, a mob formed, threw the press into the Ohio River, and started burning homes in the Little Africa section of Cincinnati. After three nights of riots, people became concerned that other businesses and homes might get damaged, so the town leaders formed groups of men to stop the rioters. It would be another twenty-five years before the Civil War broke out.

RIOT
in the
NIGHT

Bonnie Hinman

BARBOUR
PUBLISHING, INC.
Uhrichsville, Ohio

For my mother, Irene Wirts, with love.

Published by Barbour Publishing, Inc.
P.O. Box 719
Uhrichsville, Ohio 44683
www.barbourbooks.com

 Member of the
Evangelical Christian
Publishers Association

Printed in the United States of America.

Cover illustration by Peter Pagano.
Inside illustrations by Adam Wallenta.

Chapter 1
Louisa Gets Stuck

There was no sign of anyone. Or at least no sign of anyone who would recognize her. Louisa squeezed between two huge crates sitting in front of the warehouse that opened onto the Cincinnati wharf by the Ohio River. The whole wharf was jammed with crates, barrels, and sacks waiting to be loaded onto various steamboats. She stretched as tall as she could but still couldn't see the *River Queen*.

There was a ripping sound as Louisa caught her dress on a rough wooden board. She grabbed her dress to free it but didn't stop to look at the tear. That boat had to be here somewhere. Her father had talked about the grand new steamboat fresh from Pittsburgh only this morning. He'd said it was the fanciest steamboat he had ever seen, and he should know because that was his job—building steamboats. Louisa just wanted a glimpse. What could that hurt?

It must be off to the left behind all that cargo. With another quick look around for familiar faces, Louisa gathered her skirt in one hand and scrambled up and over some bags. She dropped the small cloth bag she had been carrying and climbed on the crates that were blocking her view.

One final hop put her on top of a big crate. There she balanced and scanned the riverfront for the *River Queen*. And there it was. She smiled as she stared. The boat was painted white with blue trim and sported fancy wooden scrollwork on her railings. She was a side-wheeler, with her big paddles hidden under boxes emblazoned with a huge gold crown. It was truly a queen of a steamboat.

All of a sudden, the crate Louisa was standing on shifted. In a flash she was falling, and as she went down, some other boxes and then bags came with her. Louisa didn't have time to do anything more than squeak her dismay before she came to rest under a pile of boxes and bags.

She just sat for a couple seconds. It was apparent that she hadn't been knocked unconscious, and as she mentally reviewed the condition of her limbs, she didn't think she was bleeding, either. In fact, she didn't think she was hurt at all. With a shrug of her shoulders, she began pushing the boxes back so she could climb out. That was when she realized that her left leg was firmly pinned beneath a bag of some sort of grain.

She tugged first at the bag and then at her uncooperative leg. Strong as she was for an eleven-year-old going on twelve, she couldn't budge that bag. Time for another approach. She pushed a couple more boxes out of the way and peered around them. There were other people just a little ways down the wharf. She could yell for help, and someone would hear her and come. That wasn't the problem. The problem might be who would come. Her father's shipyard was close by. One of his workers might come to rescue her, or maybe even her father would respond. That was a solution that Louisa wished to avoid.

She wasn't supposed to be down at the riverfront by herself. Girls just weren't allowed to come to such places alone. It was silly, but then lots of the rules for girls were silly. Her father was usually pretty understanding, but this time might be different. Louisa knew that her father would have brought her to see the *River Queen* if she could have waited a day or so. No, a rescue by her father was not what she wanted.

She sat there for a while and thought. Every so often she gave her leg another tug, but it was stuck fast. She wondered if it was permissible to pray for God to move the bag without the help of another person. She was sure that she could ask God for anything, but it didn't seem quite right to pray that sort of prayer, considering the circumstances. So she just prayed for help—any kind that God might send.

Just when she had decided that God must surely expect her to yell for help, Louisa was distracted by the sight of a familiar figure striding down the dock. It was Henry, her older brother. At fourteen he was tall and strong. He could surely move the bag, and even though Henry might tease her sometimes, he wasn't likely to get her in trouble. He was probably down at the Cincinnati wharf making deliveries for Dr. Drake, or maybe he was on his way to the shipyard to help their father.

"Henry!" Louisa kept her voice low, but her brother didn't pause.

She tried again, a little louder this time and certainly with more urgency. She couldn't let Henry get away. "Henry! Over here!" This time he stopped and looked around with a frown.

"Over here," Louisa repeated.

Henry started toward her, but she could tell that he still couldn't see her.

"Who's there?" he called.

"It's me," Louisa answered.

"Louisa?" Henry stood in front of his sister and stared. "What in the world are you doing?"

"Well, it's nothing for my health, that's for sure," she snapped. Her leg was starting to get numb, and Henry was asking dumb questions. "Get me out of here. I'm stuck."

"Stuck? Are you all right? How did you get stuck?"

"My leg is pinned under this bag, I'm fine, and it's a long story." Louisa whacked the bag of grain with her hand. "Please just get me out."

In seconds Henry had moved the bag and pulled Louisa out of her trap. She limped around for a minute as the blood began to circulate again in her leg. She brushed some dirt off her dress and inspected the tear.

"I thought you were going to Martha's this afternoon for

some kind of party," Henry said. "How'd you end up here at the river?"

"I just wanted to take a quick look at that steamboat that Papa was talking about. The *River Queen*. Then I was going to Martha's. I'm sure I haven't missed anything at the party." Louisa wrinkled her nose. "Unless it's more talk about the latest fabulous hairstyle from Philadelphia."

Henry laughed. "So that's how it is. They're too girly for you." He reached out and twitched her bonnet sideways a bit.

Louisa just rolled her eyes at her brother.

"Well, in any case, you're not supposed to be down here, so you'd best make tracks for Martha's lovely tea party." Henry laughed again. "I'll walk you back up to her block."

In a few minutes Louisa was safely escorted to Martha's street. Henry waved and hurried back the way they had come. She straightened her bonnet again and strolled sedately up the short sidewalk to her friend's front door.

"Louisa! Where have you been?" Martha demanded almost before she swung the door open in answer to Louisa's knock. Her brown curls bounced with each word. She reached for Louisa's bonnet.

"I was delayed, sort of." Louisa tucked a sprig of hair back behind her ear.

Martha looked at her friend more closely. "What happened? You look. . ." Martha hesitated before glancing over her shoulder into the open door of the parlor. "You haven't been fighting with Samuel Scott again, have you?"

"Martha," Louisa's voice was full of outrage. "I was seven years old when I had that fight with Samuel. I can assure you that I haven't been fighting. It was just a small mishap." She patted her hair and brushed at her skirt again.

Martha looked unconvinced but nodded and turned Louisa into the parlor. "We're all in here, of course."

Trailing behind Martha, the first thing Louisa saw was the small table with trays of little sandwiches and positively tiny cookies. And, of course, there was a tea service with cups and saucers. Oh for the days when snacks at their parties might actually fill a body up. It seemed like hours since Louisa had eaten, and now it looked like it would be more hours before she would get to eat anything substantial.

Martha's voice pulled her attention away from thoughts of hunger. "Julia, this is Louisa. Her father builds steamboats right here in Cincinnati."

Louisa stepped around Martha. Who on earth was Julia? And why would she be interested in what Louisa's father did? Louisa saw that all of the girls seemed to be gathered in a clump around the small sofa in the far corner of Martha's parlor.

In the middle of the group sat a girl whom Louisa had never seen before. She was tiny with fat black curls pulled back from a delicately lovely face. Louisa stared, even though she knew it was rude. The stranger looked older than the twelve- or thirteen-year-old girls gathered around her, and she looked somehow foreign. Actually she looked like a foreign queen, Louisa thought, with her subjects gathered around her. The queen raised her head to look at Louisa, as did the other girls who sat or stood around the settee.

"Well, I declare, Louisa. It's a pleasure to meet you. My name is Julia, Julia Garnett." The words drawled lazily from her dainty red lips. She smiled sweetly up at Louisa. "Your father builds steamboats, does he? How fascinating. So much more interesting than what my papa does."

Louisa could only nod and attempt to smile. Who was this girl? Her southern accent was more pronounced than Louisa had ever heard before. Her words were polite and even cordial, yet there was something about her. With a mental shake, Louisa found her tongue at last. "I'm pleased to meet you, too, Julia. What does your father do?" Louisa wasn't sure what fathers' occupations had to do with anything, but Julia seemed interested, and she was the new girl.

"Land's sake. My papa's a planter." The words almost seemed to drip from her mouth. "A Georgia planter."

"Oh, I see," Louisa said. She could tell by the way that the other girls were nodding and smiling and exchanging glances that they all thought that a Georgia planter was a very big deal indeed. Louisa was of the opinion that a planter was a type of farmer and was a perfectly respectable and necessary occupation. Something told her, though, that farmer wasn't the right word—or at least wouldn't be to Julia.

"So you're from Georgia," Louisa said and moved closer. "What brings you to Cincinnati?"

"We've come to visit our Aunt Cynthia for the summer, my brother Walter and I. It's just so everlastingly hot in Georgia in the summer. Papa thought we might enjoy coming north this time of year to escape the heat."

Louisa made herself concentrate on the words Julia spoke instead of the way she said them. "I hope you enjoy your stay. I'm afraid it gets pretty hot here in Cincinnati in the summer, too."

Julia laughed. It almost tinkled, but suddenly Louisa found

11

herself clenching her teeth. That laugh was not a pleasant sound.

"Well, I declare, Louisa," Julia said with another laugh. "It just couldn't be as hot as Georgia. It's a positive steam bath in August."

Louisa had her mouth open to argue the relative steaminess of August in Cincinnati when Martha interrupted. Evidently her friend had decided that enough had been said about the weather.

"We were about to get out our needlework when you came, Louisa." Martha motioned to the group. "While we stitch, Julia is going to tell us about the latest styles in the South."

Immediately the girls all hurried to pick up needlework bags from nearby chairs or tables. With a sigh of resignation, Louisa looked around for her bag. Then she remembered.

"Oh, no," she said with a barely repressed grunt of frustration.

"What's wrong?" Martha inquired. The others were already settling back into chairs as they pulled out their fancy needlework.

"I left my bag." Louisa hesitated. "Well, I just left it. That's all." She had been about to say that she left her needlework bag at the wharf on a crate. Somehow this didn't seem the time to talk about climbing on crates and getting stuck.

Julia shook out some sort of lace in her lap. She waved a tiny white hand in Louisa's direction. "Land's sake, Louisa dear, send a darkie after it."

"A darkie?" Louisa asked before she remembered that she'd rather seem more knowledgeable in front of the Georgia visitor.

"Of course." Julia nodded her head firmly. "Send a darkie to get it." She waved her hand again. "A slave, send a slave."

There was silence in the room. Louisa looked at Martha, who only raised her eyebrows slightly.

Louisa cleared her throat. "Well, Julia. . ."

Julia's laugh suddenly rang out again. "Oh, silly me. I totally forgot." She shook her head until her dark curls rippled. "You don't have any slaves. How do you get along? Such an inconvenience, to be sure."

Louisa just stood there trying to calculate what she should say. Of course they didn't have any slaves. Slavery had never been legal in Ohio. Even if it was legal, she knew that she'd still think it was wrong. Before she could get those words out or even decide if it would be polite to say them, Julia had changed the subject to the latest hairstyles. The other girls seemed relieved to abandon the discussion of retrieving Louisa's needlework bag.

With a sigh Louisa let the moment pass. She would be pleased to lose her needlework bag permanently. There might still be some good in this afternoon if she didn't have to sit and stitch at some useless bit of fancywork. That pleasant thought had barely occurred to her when a small basket was dropped into her hands.

"You can work on that this afternoon," Martha said, "so you'll have something to do. You can get your bag later."

Louisa wanted to groan, but Martha's smile, with only a touch of mischief evident, was too contagious.

Louisa smiled back and flopped in a nearby chair. "Thank you, I think," she muttered as she rummaged in the basket. Some days were better forgotten. Just then her finger met up with a loose needle in Martha's sampler. When she plunged the injured pinkie into her mouth to keep blood from staining the white muslin, her stomach growled loudly in a most unladylike fashion. That reminded her of the dainty sandwiches. And then she did groan.

CHAPTER 2
A Good Argument

Henry hurried back the way he had come after watching Louisa trudge up the walk to Martha's front door. It wasn't the first time that he had rescued his little sister from her own curiosity. She didn't much like being a girl, and even though he probably wouldn't admit it to Louisa, he didn't really blame her for chafing at the restrictions placed on girls. He knew that he wouldn't like it one bit.

Henry glanced at the clock in the nearby church tower. There was still enough time to stop by and see Abe. Abe was a school friend whose family lived ten miles away down the Ohio. It was too far for Abe to travel each day for classes, so he lived with a printer who gave Abe a free room and meals in return for Abe's help with the printing jobs. Abe worked after school and on Saturdays during the school year, and now that it was summer, he was working every day. The printer even paid him a little during the summer. Sometimes Henry felt a bit envious of his friend's freedom from family rules, but Abe said it was lonely in spite of the kindness of Mr. Pugh and his family.

Abe was out in front of the print shop, sweeping the sidewalk, when Henry arrived and tried to sneak up on his friend. "You missed a spot," Henry said sternly.

Abe jerked his broom toward Henry. "I saw you sneaking up, you river rat." He gave a final sweep with the broom. "What you up to? Anything going on in this old town?"

"Not much." Henry leaned against the door frame. "Nothing is ever going on in this town, is it?"

"Now I wouldn't exactly agree with that," Abe replied as he returned the broom to its corner. "Things have been pretty interesting around here lately."

"You mean here, in the print shop?" Henry asked. He guessed that Abe was teasing him. He couldn't think of much that was exciting happening in a print shop.

Suddenly there was a commotion at the end of the block. Both boys turned to see what was going on. Henry saw a group of men coming down the sidewalk who all seemed to be talking at once and loudly. As they came closer, he saw that in the middle of the group there was one man who appeared to be the center of attention. The gray-haired older man was striding along while the others clustered around him. It sounded more and more like a noisy argument to Henry. He strained to hear what they were saying. Henry

16

loved a good argument almost as much as he loved cherry pie. And this one sounded like a dandy.

"That's what I was talking about," Abe said and gestured toward the approaching men.

Henry was distracted from the men for a moment. "What do you mean?"

"The interesting stuff going on," Abe said and pushed his friend back away from the door.

Henry frowned. What was the connection? Before he could ask, the men reached the front of the print shop and stopped. The argument, however, continued, and Henry saw that it was the gray-haired man against the others.

"That's James Birney," Abe said in a low voice as he jabbed his finger toward the gray-haired man. "The publisher of the *Philanthropist*. Things heat up when he's around."

Henry nodded in understanding as it all started making more sense. The *Philanthropist* was an abolitionist newspaper that was printed in Mr. Pugh's shop. Mr. Birney had moved to Cincinnati in April to publish his paper that denounced slavery in no uncertain terms. Henry had heard a lot of talk about Mr. Birney but hadn't seen him before. It was funny how little this man seemed to match up with some of the descriptions Henry had heard of him. Wild-eyed fanatic didn't really seem to fit this ordinary-looking man. Granted, he was arguing loudly and with considerable passion, but he appeared normal enough. Henry admired anyone who would jump into an argument with both feet.

The boys stood, backs pressed against the front wall of the print shop, as the words flowed around them like the Ohio River during a flood.

"Birney, there's going to be big trouble if you don't shut down this newspaper." The words were practically spat out by a young, dark-haired man.

"Aye," a second older man said, "Robert is right. All this abolitionist claptrap you're printing is stirring people up."

"If that is the case, gentlemen, then I have succeeded at my task." James Birney stood calmly in the doorway of the print shop. "To stir people up, as you state it, is ever my goal. To apprise the population of the degradation to be found in the forced servitude that is slavery, that is indeed my aim." Birney's voice rose as he spoke. "Every man, be he black or white, deserves to share in the riches of this great nation."

A third man spoke up. "Mr. Birney, I think that we agree on many aspects of this problem. All of us are antislavery and wish to see that institution done away with." Henry saw that the others were nodding. "But it must be done in a way that respects the interests of all involved."

"By that, sir," Birney said, "you mean the commercial interests of Cincinnati. Those interests that desire to keep the good nature of the southern slave states that trade here in this great city."

"Well now, that is to be considered," the man replied as he bobbed his head vigorously. "But it's certainly not the only consideration."

Henry looked at a fourth man, who hadn't spoken since they had gathered in front of the print shop. He was tall and skinny and perhaps older than the others. Now he was slowly nodding his head. "Birney," he said in a deep voice, "what you're wanting would cause chaos in every town in this nation. It would mean hordes of freed slaves roaming the

18

land, ill-prepared to take care of themselves."

"That's right," a new voice yelled from the street. Henry saw that several people had stopped to listen. They were mostly men, but there was a woman or two who had stopped on the edge. The voice continued, "We don't need those black people taking our jobs. Let them go home to Africa, where they belong."

Henry heard a murmur of agreement. He waited to see if Mr. Birney would respond. Of course, Henry had heard and read about all these different ideas, but never like this. It was exciting, and while he itched to ask some questions, he knew that this probably wasn't the right time. Now if his outspoken cousin Rachel were here, she'd probably speak right up.

"My friends," James Birney's strong voice broke into Henry's thoughts as it swelled over the group, "there is no other consideration more important than the immediate release from bondage for our black brothers."

"You're no friend to us" was shouted from the street.

"And I, for one, have no brothers who are black."

"Get rid of him and his disgusting newspaper."

The crowd on the street pushed forward, and Henry felt a surge of alarm. He hadn't thought that mere words could move people so much. They seemed ready to grab Mr. Birney and bodily remove him from Cincinnati.

Yet another voice rose over the crowd. "Stop this now. Please." It came from the print shop doorway beyond where James Birney stood.

Henry saw Mr. Pugh, the printer, standing there, wiping his ink-stained hands on a rag. Henry knew that Achilles Pugh was a Quaker and as such had no toleration for violence. How

19

would he stop this crowd that now threatened Mr. Birney?

"Your words have merit as do all men's," Mr. Pugh said, "yet this method of expression can only lead to disaster." The crowd settled immediately as his measured words reached them. "Please, go on about your business. We must all gather at a better time and in a more comfortable setting to discuss these issues." The printer finished speaking and just stood there quietly, watching the others.

In a few moments, Henry was surprised to see the older man from the original group shrug his shoulders and turn to go. There was a rumble of dissatisfaction, but the crowd quickly slipped away. Mr. Birney shook Mr. Pugh's hand and followed the printer back into the print shop.

Henry turned to Abe. "I see what you mean now. Interesting stuff does happen when Mr. Birney is around."

"I guess I haven't talked to you lately," Abe said. "This sort of thing has been happening more and more often. Who would have thought that Mr. Pugh's taking over the printing of the *Philanthropist* in April could lead to so much excitement? I better go. There may be deliveries for me to make."

Henry nodded and watched his friend go back inside the shop. Then he headed down the street. The thoughts were bouncing around in his head like popcorn over a fire. There was much to think about. There was always a lot of talk in Cincinnati about any and every subject, but somehow this seemed different to Henry. He had been taught from childhood that slavery was wrong but had never really considered all the possible problems in getting rid of it.

Soon he was back in Dr. Drake's office, where he straightened up and replenished supplies so all would be ready when the doctor came in that evening to see some patients. He loved helping Dr. Drake both in his medical practice and with the observations the doctor kept of natural events such as weather and the river level. Henry had known for a long time that he wanted to be a doctor someday, and Dr. Drake was the best teacher ever.

Finally he finished and started for home. There was just about enough time to do his chores and check the Ohio River level for his records before supper.

"Henry! Where are you going in such a hurry?"

Henry looked over his shoulder to see that his friend Raleigh was just coming out of a nearby store. Raleigh's brown hair was slicked down, and he looked sort of dressed up for a summer afternoon. Then Henry saw that there was another boy with Raleigh. He was tall like Henry with blond hair, but the stranger's hair was long and straight instead of short and curly.

"Raleigh," Henry yelled. Then he trotted back to walk with his friend and the other boy. "How have you been? I haven't seen you since school let out. I went by your house a couple times, but you weren't there."

"I had to go with my mother and sister to Pittsburgh to visit my grandmother." Raleigh rolled his eyes. "Did I miss anything?"

Henry ignored his question and gave his friend a look that was meant to ask who this stranger was. Raleigh looked momentarily puzzled, but then understanding dawned.

"You two haven't met," he said and stopped short. "Walter, this is my friend Henry. Henry, this is Walter Garnett. He's visiting his aunt, who's friends with my grandmother.

We met in Pittsburgh."

Walter held out his hand to Henry, who quickly stepped forward to shake it. "It's a pleasure to meet you, Henry."

Walter's words were formal, but that wasn't what made Henry struggle not to stare. The stranger had the broadest southern drawl that Henry had ever heard. Henry had no doubt that this boy came from the Deep South. "Me, too," Henry managed to reply and then added, "You must come from the South." Henry resisted a strong urge to comment on the boy's accent. Walter looked a little bored, politely bored to be sure, but bored all the same.

"Yes, I come from Georgia," Walter drawled. "Down near Atlanta."

"You're a long ways from home. Are you enjoying your visit?"

Walter smiled but didn't answer for a moment. "Cincinnati is quite a change. I haven't traveled this far west before."

Walter made Cincinnati sound like it was so far west that it was east.

Walter continued, "The pigs are a novelty. In Georgia we pen up our swine." He chuckled. "It's quite a sight here to see the pigs running in the streets."

"My father says there aren't nearly as many as there used to be," Raleigh said.

"Most people keep them fenced in nowadays, but some old-timers still let their pigs out to forage on garbage. Dr. Drake says it's not a safe way to get rid of rubbish." Henry knew he must sound kind of preachy, but Walter was rubbing him the wrong way. Henry had to admit, however, that he had often made fun of the pigs that still grunted their way through the gutters. He just didn't want Walter to do it.

"We'll walk with you, Henry," Raleigh said. "I don't have to do my chores this evening since Walter is here."

Henry shrugged and grinned. "You can help me with my chores if you're feeling deprived."

"Thanks," Raleigh said, "but I think I can survive." The three boys started walking toward Henry's street. "Back to my first question. Did I miss anything while I was gone?"

"Nothing much," Henry replied. "But earlier this afternoon I did run into a little excitement." Henry told the story of the confrontation in front of the print shop as the boys hurried along.

"I wish I had been there," Raleigh said. "Did you think the crowd might really do something to Mr. Birney?"

"Not at first, but then I began to wonder," Henry said. "They seemed really angry at him."

"I'm not surprised." Walter spoke up for the first time. "I've heard of that nut, James Birney. He's almost as bad as that Garrison fellow. Abolitionists are all fanatics. They should be shipped off to Africa along with the free blacks."

Henry looked up, startled by Walter's strong words. Raleigh frowned and quickly changed the subject. Henry didn't say anything but allowed himself a tiny smile of satisfaction. He sensed a good argument coming and was disappointed when Raleigh hustled Walter on down the street after they'd reached Henry's house. Oh well, there'd surely be another chance to match wits with the southern boy.

CHAPTER 3
Julia Speaks Up

"Do you want these preserves in each basket?" Louisa asked her mother, who was counting out eggs. The two of them were packing food baskets for several families who lived a few blocks away. The father in one family had been laid up with a broken leg for three weeks, and another family had lost most of their belongings in a fire. The rest of the baskets were for the "regulars," as Mama called them. They were families with only a mother taking care of several children, and there were a couple of elderly women with no grown children to help them.

"Yes," Louisa's mother said, "I think there are plenty to put one in every basket." She finished doling out the eggs. "We must remember to ask Rachel and Betsy to bring extra eggs next market day. And they should have some blackberries before long, I think." Mama bent over the big kitchen table to tuck napkins in the finished baskets. "It's almost time for fresh corn and beans, too. But this talk of food is making me hungry. How about you?"

"I'm always hungry," Louisa said. It was true. Sometimes Louisa wondered if there was something wrong with her. Her friends thought she had an unbelievable appetite and a very unladylike love of food. At least her mother didn't seem concerned. She just said that Louisa was a healthy, growing girl. Louisa shook off thoughts of food to ask her mother a question. "May I go with you to deliver baskets today?"

Her mother frowned briefly. "Let's see. Let me think a minute about where they're going." She stared at the baskets as if trying to see the path she would take to deliver each one. "You could come to Mrs. Bennett's house with me and certainly to Miss Emma's. Miss Emma would love to see you. I'll go there later just to visit her. She doesn't need a food basket, just some company."

Louisa sighed. She loved Miss Emma, who had been a family friend for years, but that wasn't how she wanted to help her mother. "Could I go with you to the Richardsons or the Petersons?"

"Louisa, you know I don't like you to go to those kinds of homes. They aren't clean, and they just aren't a very good place for you to be. I'm afraid of disease. There has been

25

some sickness in both households lately."

"Why don't they keep their houses clean?" Louisa asked.

It was her mother's turn to sigh. "They do the best they can with what they have to work with. There are several people crowded into a small space, and they have to carry water quite a distance. The houses themselves are more aptly called shacks. Their floors are often rotten, and the walls are damp and moldy."

Mama shook her head. "Right now, for one reason or another, they just can't afford any better housing. I'm hoping that with a little help they may eventually be able to move to bigger quarters."

"I'd like to help, too," Louisa said. She knew that there would be something that she might do to help these families if she could go along.

"I know that, and if I thought it was safe, I'd certainly take you." Louisa's mother came around the table and gave her daughter a hug. "You're a good worker. I'd be foolish not to take you along if I dared."

"I bet you'd take Henry if he wanted to go," Louisa ventured.

"Why do you say that?" Mama kept her hands on Louisa's shoulders as she talked.

"Because he's a boy, that's why," Louisa blurted out.

"Oh, I see. So that's how it is." Mama released Louisa and turned to pick up a couple of baskets. "I don't think that's true at all. I would never have let Henry go somewhere that I thought was dangerous when he was your age. He's older now and allowed to make more of his own decisions, but that has nothing to do with him being a boy."

Louisa's mother started through the house with the baskets over her arm. "I understand that you find the restrictions of being a girl unbearable sometimes, Louisa, and often I agree." She stopped for a moment and smiled at her daughter. "Just remember that God has placed each one of us here on this earth for a purpose, both men and women. You just have to find yours. God will help you in that search if you let Him. I'll be back before dinnertime. Why don't you help Anna with the meal?"

Louisa watched her mother go down the hall and out the front door with her arms loaded down. Her mother made everything sound so easy, but it wasn't. Louisa was sure of that. Just then Anna, the woman who helped out in the Lankford home, came bustling in the back door with a big basket over her arm. Back from shopping, she'd be starting the noon meal soon. Louisa could help with that, but it didn't sound very interesting.

"What's the matter with you, child?" Anna inquired in her loud voice. "You look as low as a worm on a hook."

Louisa couldn't help smiling. Anna did have a way with words. "I was wanting to go with Mama to deliver baskets, but she said it wasn't safe."

"Well then, if your mother says it's so, it must be. I've seldom known her to be wrong." Anna grabbed her big apron off the hook and began to pull bowls and spoons and other utensils out of the cupboards. "Besides, those poor people don't need you there gawking at their misfortune. They've got trouble enough as it is."

"I wouldn't do that," Louisa said hotly.

The woman paused for a moment and looked at Louisa.

"No, I reckon you wouldn't, at that. Perhaps you'll be able to go next time." She pointed at the other apron hanging from the hook. "Meanwhile, help me here. I've been going to teach you the finer points of biscuit making, and this is as good a time as any. Can't catch a husband if you can't make good biscuits."

"I'm not looking for a husband." Louisa tied her apron with a jerk. Of all the crazy ideas.

"Well, not yet," Anna conceded. "Maybe we could just aim for biscuits good enough to put in the baskets next time."

Louisa nodded and went to stand by Anna's elbow.

That afternoon, when she was strolling sedately down the sidewalk of her neighborhood with Martha and Julia and some other girls, Louisa found herself wishing she was back cooking with Anna. Anna might be a tad opinionated and unafraid to express those opinions at length, but she was funny and clever. Working with her was always entertaining, even if it was work. Louisa scuffed her shoes lightly on the brick sidewalk. This group of giggling girls she was trailing was much less entertaining.

"Julia, tell us more about the parties you have at your plantation," Martha said. "Do you have a big ballroom?"

"Oh my, yes," Julia said. She twirled the frilly little parasol that she was carrying. "Why, I've seen as many as fifteen couples dance in our ballroom."

"That must be something to see," Miranda said in an awestruck voice.

"Indeed it is," Julia agreed. "The fine ball gowns and the

28

music and the fragrant flowers make quite a picture, and that doesn't take into account the handsome young men everywhere."

At this the girls all giggled. Except for Louisa, who just rolled her eyes and dropped farther behind the group. The afternoon in front of her had looked so endless earlier when she had agree to join her friends. She wasn't sure what she had thought they might do, but strolling up and down through the neighborhood while discussing fashion and dances was not it.

"So, Louisa," Julia turned to say, "what kind of dances do you like to do here in Cincinnati?" Her words were syrupy sweet, but Louisa wasn't fooled. There was an edge to the southerner's voice.

"Actually, Julia," Louisa responded earnestly, "I'm right fond of the Irish jig. My cousin Timothy taught it to me. He learned it from his father, who learned it from an old Irish sailor. Timothy's father was impressed into the British navy for years when he was young, you know." She smiled sweetly in spite of the dirty look Martha was giving her.

"I declare, Louisa, you're putting me on. The Irish jig, indeed," Julia said with a trill of her irritating laugh. "Those Irish are just so vulgar."

Martha gave Louisa a warning look, but it wouldn't have stopped Louisa from giving a rousing demonstration of the Irish jig right there on the sidewalk if they hadn't been interrupted.

Something thudded on the brick sidewalk behind them. Just as Louisa turned to investigate, two small boys came flying at the girls, running full tilt. Louisa reached out and grabbed the shirt of one as he tried to run past.

"What's going on here?" she demanded. "What are you running from?" The little boy was six or seven years old and wiggled in her grasp like a cornered snake.

"Not doin' nothin'," the boy croaked as he wiggled even harder. At last he managed to twist out of Louisa's grasp and race down the sidewalk to join his friend, who was almost out of sight.

Then Louisa turned back again and saw that a young black woman had evidently fallen while carrying an armload of packages. The two running boys made Louisa suspicious that the woman might have been tripped.

In a flash Louisa ran back to the woman. "Are you hurt? Did those boys trip you?" The woman rose to her knees and attempted to gather her scattered parcels.

"No, miss, I'm not hurt. Except for my dignity, I guess." She continued to pick up the packages. "The boys and I collided. I don't think they meant to trip me. We just didn't see each other."

"They could have stopped to help you up at least." Louisa looked down the street after the boys, who were out of sight now. The ornery little toads.

"Oh, they're just boys, miss."

Louisa suddenly realized that her friends hadn't followed her back to help. She looked up the sidewalk and saw that they were still standing in the same place. Martha had a worried look on her face, but the others seemed unaware or at least were pretending to be unaware that anything was amiss. If the amount of giggling was any gauge, then Julia was telling them yet another of her plantation stories. Louisa turned back to help the woman stand up.

"You have too much to carry," Louisa said. "May I help you?"

"Thank you, miss. You've been such a help already, but I can manage if you'd just put that last package on top of the others."

Louisa carefully balanced one last item on top of the stack in the woman's arms.

"Thank you so much."

"You're welcome," Louisa said with a smile. "Take your time with that load."

"I will," the woman promised and hurried off down the sidewalk, passing the other girls, who still ignored her.

Louisa walked slowly toward her friends. This whole episode just didn't feel right. It wasn't like Martha to ignore someone who might have been hurt, even if that person was a black woman. Louisa frowned as she looked at the group again.

"Was she hurt?" Martha whispered when Louisa walked up beside her. The other girls continued to chatter.

"Why are you whispering?" Louisa demanded. Without waiting for Martha to answer, she continued in a normal voice, "She was fine, no thanks to those pesky little boys."

"Louisa, what a droll character you are." To Louisa's ears Julia's drawl had a hint of steel in it, even though she smiled sweetly.

"Why, thank you, Julia." Louisa ignored the tone and responded to the words. "Although I'm not sure what droll means." She gave Julia the most innocent look she could muster.

31

Julia's cornflower blue eyes narrowed briefly before she turned to lead the group briskly down the sidewalk. "I declare," she said, "Cincinnati's atmosphere is just so western."

"What do you mean?" Miranda inquired.

"Oh, it's nothing, really," Julia said and gave her parasol an extra twirl.

"Please, tell us what you mean," Miranda said. "We're interested." The other two girls, Sally and Addie, nodded their agreement vigorously, but Martha just frowned.

"Oh, very well," Julia said and swept regally to a halt. "It's just that in Georgia and in other places I've visited, it really isn't acceptable to associate with black people."

"How do you manage your slaves if you can't associate with them?" Louisa didn't even pretend to be polite. With the exception of Martha, the girls gave Louisa displeased glares. Martha looked more worried than ever.

"I'm speaking of public association, of course," Julia said. Her usual smile faded for less than a moment before being turned once again on the group around her.

"You're speaking of ignoring someone lying on the ground, I assume." Louisa moved directly in front of Julia and stood with her hands clasped behind her back.

Julia stopped short and lowered her parasol. "Oh, pish," she said airily, "those blacks are hardy souls. I knew right away that there was nothing wrong with her." She let her laugh tinkle over her companions once more. "Why, she probably tripped over her own feet. Come along, girls. Let's go back to my Aunt Cynthia's for some cake." That said, Julia swept away down the sidewalk trailed by Miranda, Addie, and Sally.

Louisa turned her outraged eyes on Martha, who hadn't followed the others. Martha put her hands up and shook her head.

"I know, I know," she said. "She's an idiot." Martha glanced at the retreating figures. "But I have to be nice to her. My mother is a good friend of her Aunt Cynthia's."

Louisa repressed a strong urge to shake her fist at Julia's back. She knew what her mother would think of that response. "She's just so irritating. How can she be so, well, so unchristian?"

"I'm sure I don't know," Martha replied. "But my mother says that lots of people who go to church every Sunday still believe in slavery, even still own slaves."

"I wonder how that can be?" Louisa said. Her anger drained away, leaving her puzzled. "It seems like the Bible is pretty clear on that point. Jesus died to save everyone and that surely has to include black people, doesn't it?"

"I don't see how it could mean anything else, but I guess it could be one of those things that we aren't supposed to understand until we get to heaven," Martha said.

"No, I don't think so," Louisa said. "But that doesn't mean I understand it. Let's go. I'm hungry." Louisa took her friend's arm and turned her around. "Let's go to my house. We can talk Anna out of something to eat." Perhaps two or three thick slices of bread spread with Anna's spicy sweet apple butter would help her figure all this out. It couldn't hurt.

CHAPTER 4
The Infernal Regions

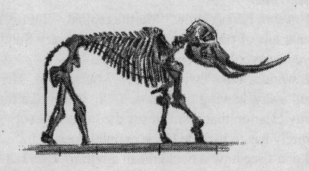

"I heard that they've brought back the Invisible Girl exhibit at the Western Museum," Abe said as he and Henry walked out on the Lankfords' front porch. "Do you want to go there?"

Henry looked at the rain that poured down in buckets. "Sounds like a first-rate idea. It's probably been a year since I've been there. Can you afford it?"

"Sure can," Abe said with gusto. "Mr. Pugh paid me today. Said I was the best worker he'd ever had. How about you? Any money?"

"Enough," Henry replied. "My father paid me, too, although he didn't say anything about me being his best worker."

Abe laughed. "I'm sure that goes without saying."

"Come on, you liar. Let's see if we can dodge these raindrops," Henry said.

They had planned to go fishing on this Saturday afternoon in June, but Henry wasn't all that interested in standing out in the rain if there was something else to do. The Western Museum was perfect.

"I don't think there's any dodging drops in this deluge," Abe said. The pair took off running, and it wasn't long before they were standing in the vestibule of the museum, attempting to shake the excess water off their clothes. In a few moments they had paid the admission fee and were inside.

"What first?" Henry asked his friend.

"You pick," Abe said. "I don't know my way around. I've only been here once before. My pa brought me when I was twelve. He said that Ma wasn't likely to approve so we'd best keep quiet about it."

"Yeah, my mother says it's a little gory for her taste," Henry said.

"That's part of the fun," Abe said.

Henry laughed and nodded his agreement. "Want to start off with some of the old standbys and work our way up to the Invisible Girl and the Infernal Regions?"

"Good plan," Abe agreed. "I want to see that New Zealand chief's tattooed head and the strange mirrors, too."

The boys went off to wander among the rooms, which

housed woolly mammoth bones in one corner and wax figures depicting the death of George Washington in another. One room was full of mirrors that distorted the boys' images, making them look either short and squat or tall and thin.

"I had forgotten how many wax figures there are," Abe said after awhile.

"I know. Have you noticed how all these wax figure scenes show something sad or violent?" Henry motioned at the one in front of them. It showed a man collapsing as he was stabbed with a dagger by a woman. He wasn't sure if the expressions were lifelike, but they sure were vivid.

"You're right," Abe said. They moved on to look at the chief's tattooed head. "Has the museum always had all this stuff? You know, the wax figures and the head and all that?"

"That's the only way I remember it," Henry said as he peered at the shriveled head that hardly looked like a head anymore. "But my father says it used to be just a regular museum with bones and fossils and other scientific objects."

"What happened?"

"Didn't make enough money," Henry replied. "So the curator, the head guy, started putting in all these weird and freaky things."

"And that made money?" Abe asked.

"It must have, because it's still around." Henry moved on. "I guess people would rather pay to see this kind of exhibit." He pointed at a bandit scene in front of them that was particularly lurid.

"I know I would," Abe said. "Let's go see the Invisible Woman now."

"Henry! Abe!" A familiar voice called from behind the

boys. Henry turned to see that it was Raleigh with Walter close behind.

"I didn't know you were coming here today, Henry," Raleigh said.

"We didn't, either," Henry said. "The rain made it seem like a better idea than going fishing." He looked at Walter, who was peering around with interest on his face instead of the bored expression of the other day. "What do you think of the Western Museum, Walter?"

"Rather amusing, if you like this sort of thing," Walter drawled.

"We do," Henry said promptly. He turned his head so he could roll his eyes without Walter seeing it. This southern boy had a way of irritating a body without half trying. But the good manners that Henry's mother had been at pains to teach him kept Henry from being as rude as he felt like being.

"Going to see the Invisible Woman?" Raleigh asked.

"That's next," Abe answered. "Want to come with us?"

"Sure," Raleigh agreed, "let's go."

The large chamber that housed the Invisible Woman was dark except for filtered light that came from behind some filmy painted backdrops. There were wax figures in the shadows depicting, Henry thought, a scene from one of Shakespeare's plays, something with witches. But the center of attention was what looked like a cloud in the middle of the room.

"Look at that," Abe whispered. "It's a hand coming out of the cloud."

Henry whispered back. "The cloud has to be fake, but the

37

hand looks real, and it's holding something."

"It's a trumpet," said Raleigh as they crowded in beside several other people. "For delivering her messages. Sam Cook told me about it."

Just then someone in the front of the group spoke up to ask a question. After a pause, a voice seemed to come from the trumpet, giving an answer in a high-pitched tone. This happened several times before an attendant herded the group from the chamber so another contingent of eager questioners could enter.

"What idiot would believe that was real?" Walter asked as soon as they were back out in the hallway.

"It's not real?" Abe asked. His voice rose almost to a squeak.

For a moment Henry thought his friend was serious, but then he got a better look at Abe's face. The mischief was plainly written there, and Henry started laughing. Soon Raleigh joined in, and even Walter mustered a lazy grin.

"Come on you clown," Henry said and grabbed Abe's arm. "Let's take Walter to see the Infernal Regions exhibit." If it was possible to stir an honest reaction from Walter, the Infernal Regions might do it.

"Let's go," Raleigh said. "It's really something, Walter. Sort of literary. You'll like it."

"Literary?" Walter's question was almost a snort of disbelief.

"Raleigh's right." Henry clapped his old friend on the back. "It's based on Dante's *Divine Comedy*. You know, the book about heaven and hell."

"This is mostly about the hell part," Abe said. "Dante

called it the Inferno."

"I'm aware of that," Walter snapped.

The visitor's drawl almost vanished when he was irritated, Henry observed to himself. "Here we are," he said aloud and stopped in front of the door of a large chamber.

Together the four boys went into the dark room to join several other visitors who were already peering through the grate of iron bars that screened the scenes beyond. Henry waited a few moments for his eyes to adjust to the dim light. He found a spot in front of the grate and motioned for the others to move up.

They all stared at the eerie scene before them. In the middle of the room was an elevated throne. On it, in horrible splendor, sat a wax representation of the devil himself. He was dressed in a sable robe and held a pitchfork in his hand. He wore a huge crown, and his face was partially covered by a bristly beard that looked to Henry's critical eyes like it had recently been part of a horse's tail. His head was constructed to nod at the spectators while his eyes rolled in a menacing fashion. Henry gave an involuntary shudder. Even though he knew it was all just tricks and wax and such, it was still a frightening sight.

Henry turned to look at Walter. The southern boy looked intently at the scene. It was hard to judge his reaction, but Henry calculated that Walter wasn't finding Cincinnati quite so dull right now.

Suddenly there was a loud groaning noise that made Henry jump. It was followed by various other noises of intense suffering. He had forgotten about the sound effects that accompanied the scenes. The noises drew his attention to the scene to the right of the devil's throne.

"Look," he ordered Walter, who obediently turned his eyes right. According to the sign displayed in front, this was the hell of fire. Wax skeletons were thrown about and there was a general air of fire consuming everything. The sockets of the eyes of the skeletons were filled with some substance that made them glow as if on fire. More of the substance produced a lake of fire from which rose fearsome-looking creatures.

After a few minutes, the crowd shifted, and the boys moved slightly so they could view the scene to the left of the throne. It was labeled the hell of ice. This department of hell showed the doomed as frozen. The wax figures were clearly men, women, and children frozen fast among mountains of ice.

Henry noticed one frozen figure that he hadn't seen on other visits—perhaps because he had been apt to hide his eyes when he was younger. It was a wax figure of an old black man. Wide, horrified eyes stared out above a mouth that was open in a perpetual frozen scream. Henry shivered as he stared at the old man. It almost felt cold, although common sense told him that it was quite stuffy and hot.

"Let's go," he said and nudged Abe, who obligingly turned to leave. Just then the crowd pressed forward again as some new spectators in the back tried to get in a better position. There was a slight scuffling as someone in the front was caught off balance and shoved up against the protective grate. In less than a second, a shock passed smartly through the crowd, and there was a general outcry. Body parts touching each other in the crowded room tingled and jumped uncomfortably. Quickly the crowd backed away. There was murmuring as the majority, including the four boys, made their way out of the Infernal Regions.

"What was that?" Walter demanded as soon as they reached the hallway.

"You mean the shock?" Abe led the way toward the front of the museum.

"Of course I mean the shock or whatever it was." Once again Walter's irritation caused his drawl to fade.

"It was an electric shock," Henry answered. "They use a machine to pass an electrical current through wires on the back side of that grate. If someone puts his hand through the bars either accidentally or on purpose, he gets a shock. The current passes from person to person if they are touching."

"But why?" Walter asked. The boys had reached the front door of the museum to see that the rain had stopped at last.

"My father said it started out to keep the big crowds of people from trying to get closer to the wax figures," Henry said. "I kind of think it's just for the effect now. I've only felt it once before. How about you, Raleigh?"

Raleigh laughed. "I was never this close to the front before. The current gets weaker as it goes through more people. Sure did make me jerk."

"I think it's uncivilized," Walter said as they started down the sidewalk, dodging puddles every other step.

Henry shrugged. "I imagine it's harmless enough. So what did you think of the Infernal Regions, Walter? Have anything like it in Georgia?"

"Can't say that we do." His accent had returned. "It was different. I'll give you that. Some of it was pretty funny. That old slave in the ice hell really entertained me. I've seen them look that way lots of times."

"You don't say," Henry said mildly.

"Sure," Walter said, "when they think they're going to get the whip."

"So you have slaves in Georgia?" Abe asked.

"How else could we run the plantation?" Walter answered. "In fact, we have at least a hundred slaves."

Abe whistled. "That many? That's a lot, isn't it?"

"We have a big plantation," Walter said. "It takes dozens of workers in the cotton fields, and then there's the house and gardens and barns."

"Couldn't you hire workers?" Henry asked. He felt an argument brewing.

Walter stopped at a street corner before crossing. "Why would we want to do that? Slaves are better workers for the cotton fields, anyhow."

"And a lot cheaper, too," Henry said. The Georgia boy spoke with such contempt that Henry was about to forget his manners.

Raleigh spoke up before Walter could respond. "Abe, I bet your Mr. Birney wouldn't like to hear about Walter's slaves."

"No, I expect not," Abe agreed.

"Like I said the other day," Walter said, "Mr. Birney is a fanatic. He and those other abolitionists want to turn all the slaves loose."

"I'm sure you disagree," Henry said.

"I would think so." Walter brushed an invisible speck from his shirt sleeve. "Those slaves are property, bought and paid for. Our Constitution doesn't say a thing about taking a man's property."

"Some people would say that slaves, being humans, can't be property," said Henry.

"They'd be wrong," Walter said firmly. "Slaves may be human, but they aren't like white men."

Henry raised his eyebrows. "Is that a Christian way of looking at that?" Even as he asked his question, he knew that it wasn't a Christian viewpoint or at least not one he'd ever been taught. "I mean, Jesus helped everyone, no matter their color. He thought they were all important."

Walter shrugged his shoulders and started walking again. "The Bible is full of stories about slaves. Slavery was common then."

Henry frowned. Walter was right on that point. "Maybe it was common," he said at last, "but I'm not so sure it was acceptable." Henry fell into step beside Walter. "It sounds like a terrible life to me."

"Huh," Walter snorted. "They have everything provided for them: food, clothing, medical care. Why, our slaves are happy and wouldn't want to live any other way."

"So why do you have to whip them? If they love it so much, that is," Henry added.

"That doesn't happen often. My father only whips them when they try to run away."

"They try to run away from this place they love so much?" Henry stopped because they had reached the end of his street.

"They're not too smart, either," Walter said. "Come on, Raleigh. We need to get back to my aunt's. Thanks for an interesting afternoon, men." Walter turned left on a side street. Raleigh grimaced at his friends but followed Walter.

Henry stood for a moment, watching their retreating backs. "Well, Abe," he said and turned to his friend, "I'm so pleased that we could contribute to Walter's entertainment this afternoon."

"I heartily concur, Henry." Abe swept his cap off his head in an exaggerated bow.

Henry laughed. Enough serious thought for one afternoon. The late afternoon sun was coming out after the rain. Maybe they still had time to go fishing.

CHAPTER 5
Wax Fruit and Velvet Painting

Louisa sat herself down on the front steps of her house with Henry's dog, Jackson. It was only ten o'clock in the morning, and already she was looking for something to occupy herself besides stroking Jackson's soft ears. Of course, she knew her mother would gladly oblige her desire to keep busy with some extra chores, but that wasn't what she had in mind. No, she wanted to do something more important than snapping green beans or mending sheets. Something that counted for something.

She was distracted by a flash of skirts on the sidewalk. It was Martha, and she was moving much more quickly than usual as she rounded Louisa's gate.

"Splendid, you're here," the out-of-breath girl announced as she bounced to a stop in front of Louisa.

"Good morning," Louisa said with a laugh. "Indeed, I am very much here. How about yourself?"

"Now don't tease," Martha said severely but let a grin lift the corners of her mouth. "I've come to invite you to my house this afternoon."

"What's the occasion?" Louisa asked. The stitching session the previous week was still fresh in her mind. Spending another afternoon like that held less appeal to her than snapping beans or mending sheets.

"It's so exciting." Martha's face was shining with excitement. "Say you'll come."

"Come to what?" Louisa asked again.

"We're forming a society. It will be so exciting." Martha repeated and turned to go.

"Wait!" Louisa shoved Jackson over and jumped up. "Who is we? What kind of society?" Martha was already walking briskly down the sidewalk.

"Oh, Sally and Miranda and Addie, and, of course, Julia. It was her idea." Martha waved. "I have to hurry. Come this afternoon at one."

"What kind of society, Martha?"

"A self-improvement society," Martha called as she disappeared down the street.

Louisa flopped back down on the steps. A self-improvement society? She frowned as she thought. What did that mean? It could be something horrid like studying the latest hairstyles or learning a new way to make lace trim. But on the other hand, it might be something fun or at least bearable. Could it be worse than sitting around all day? Maybe, but she'd chance it this time.

Louisa was at Martha's door promptly at one o'clock. Her mother had insisted that she change her dress and put on her bonnet. The other girls were arriving also, and Martha ushered them into the parlor. Louisa sighed when she saw the tea table set up once again with tiny cookies and what looked like lettuce sandwiches.

This time she had taken the precaution of eating an extra large dinner so she could subsist for the afternoon without further nourishment. Her family had noticed her large appetite at dinner. Henry had muttered about gluttony being a sin. Her parents just laughed and told Henry to leave his sister to her dinner.

"Let's get started, girls," Martha said. Julia once again sat on the sofa, and the other girls pulled up chairs so they could sit around her. Louisa sat farther away in what looked to be the most comfortable chair in the room, although that wasn't saying much. Parlor furniture just wasn't made for comfort.

Everyone looked expectantly at Martha until she, too, stopped her fussing and sat down near Julia. Seeing everyone's eyes on her, she blushed and turned to Julia. "Tell them your ideas."

"Goodness sake," Julia said in her honeyed voice. "I can't take all the credit. My Aunt Cynthia was telling me about all the wonderful societies you have here in Cincinnati. She said there was a society for every cause and occasion, and it was all the rage to belong to several."

The girls nodded almost in unison. Louisa chewed her lip briefly as she thought. It was true about all the societies. Her parents belonged to at least a couple that she could think of. She thought they were relief organizations. But she also knew that Henry's friend Dr. Drake had some kind of literary society that met at his house. Was Julia talking about that kind of society?

Addie asked the question for her. "What kind of society should we start?"

"Well, of course, it must be a self-improvement society as Martha mentioned," said Julia. "One in which we could learn new things and polish the accomplishments we already have."

"So you were thinking of a literary group?" Louisa asked. "We would read books and discuss them and maybe write papers?" Even as she said this it didn't seem too likely or even terribly interesting, but anything would be better than sitting around all summer.

Julia's tinkling laughter filled the parlor. "Oh, no, Louisa dear. We would never want to be considered bluestockings."

"What's a bluestocking?" Miranda asked.

"It's a girl who reads too many books and is too smart to suit some men," Louisa piped up. This issue had been discussed at her house recently. Her father had said that he allowed as how women should get all the education they could. That might mean going to school longer or it might mean reading books or discussing issues.

Her mother had just smiled and said that men needed all the help they could get in figuring out the problems of the world.

"Now, Louisa, don't be so extreme," Julia said. "I was just thinking that our society could be a little more fun than reading stuffy books."

Louisa couldn't actually argue with that statement, although Julia made her feel like arguing with everything. "So what will we do?" Louisa asked pointedly.

"I was thinking that we might learn a couple new skills to start with. My aunt says that making wax fruit is very popular right now as an entertainment for young ladies. She also mentioned painting on velvet as an elegant pastime." Julia put her hand to her head casually. "I happen to have some experience in painting on velvet, and my aunt will teach us how to make wax fruit."

The girls all started to talk excitedly. Julia answered questions about her prowess at velvet painting and relayed what her aunt had said about making fruit out of beeswax.

"Wait, wait!" Louisa demanded as she jumped out of her chair. "Couldn't we do something that helps other people, too?" She looked around at the group. Julia looked slightly annoyed at the interruption, and Martha had on her worried look again. "Maybe in addition to the wax fruit and velvet painting." She couldn't believe she had said that. Wax fruit and velvet painting, indeed. But she'd endure both activities if they could do something else, too.

"What did you have in mind?" Julia asked with a slight smile that didn't strike Louisa as being particularly sincere.

"Maybe we could raise money for the poor children in the neighborhood. Some of them barely get enough to eat."

"Louisa, dear, even the Bible says that the poor are always with us. They just can't manage their money."

Louisa could feel her face getting red as anger rolled over her like a log tumbling downstream.

Julia continued, "Anyhow, there are tons of societies to help the poor. Our efforts wouldn't make any difference." The other girls nodded in agreement.

Louisa took a deep breath and managed to count to three before speaking. "But sometimes," she made herself speak in a calm voice, "they just need a little help. Perhaps we could collect food." She wanted to snort her displeasure. The idea, that poor people just couldn't handle their money. As if they had any money to handle.

"I think that's a good idea," Martha said.

"But girls," Julia said, "we already have the most exciting plans." A small frown creased her delicate forehead.

Louisa just looked at her, wishing the Georgia girl would say something else outrageous. Maybe the others would see through her charm then. But Julia took a deep breath, and the frown faded.

"Well, whatever you girls think," she said. "Charitable works are always important. Perhaps we will have some time for that sort of thing. But first let's plan for our other activities. Shall we start with wax fruit or velvet painting?"

The subject changed as Miranda, Sally, and Addie all began voicing their opinions about the schedule of self-improvement. Louisa looked at Martha, who just looked back with a slight shrug of her shoulders.

Louisa sank back in her chair. Of all the things for Julia to come up with, how had she managed to pick wax fruit making? Painting on velvet was almost as bad. And it was easy to see that Julia didn't intend for there to be any time for so-called charitable works. Louisa sighed and felt a stab of longing for the way things had been in other summers. The girls had played together under the trees in Martha's back-yard and in Louisa's attic. They had made up games and played all the old ones until they stumbled home tired and dirty to hear their mothers' mild complaints about unladylike behavior. It was all different now, and Louisa didn't like it one bit.

By early the next morning, Louisa was feeling more cheerful. She was off to the market with her mother to buy food and see her cousins, who came in from their country farm to sell produce.

Sometimes it was just her older cousin Rachel who drove the wagon in on market day. Rachel's younger brother, Calvin, who was just a year older than Louisa, used to come along, but lately he had been needed on the farm. Louisa missed him. Calvin was always ready to sneak away from his sister and join Louisa in exploring the marketplace stalls and wagons.

Today was no exception as Calvin wasn't with his sister and mother, but nothing could take away Louisa's pleasure at being out among the bustling tradespeople and farmers who sold dozens of different items there in the marketplace. It was the one place where no one was likely to remind her to be a lady. Everyone was too busy to notice her. It gave a nice feeling of freedom to a bright June morning.

Louisa left her mother to visit with Aunt Betsy and Rachel and went off to look around. She was supposed to be looking to see if any of the farmers had brought in cherries yet, but that left a lot of leeway for just looking.

And looking was what she was doing a few minutes later when she tripped over the tongue of a wagon that seemed to appear out of nowhere to grab her foot. She threw out her arms to catch something, anything, to break her fall. What she grabbed was some kind of cloth, and while it didn't stop her from tumbling to the ground, it did slow her down. From her heap on the ground, Louisa peered up to see that the cloth was attached to a woman. Actually it was the woman's skirt, and the woman herself was looking down at Louisa first with surprise and then concern.

"Are you all right, child?" The rather stout woman knelt down beside Louisa with surprising speed for her size. "Goodness but you took quite a spill."

Louisa gathered her wits and her skirts and sat up. "I'm fine, ma'am, I think." She rubbed her elbows, which were a little scraped, but otherwise she was in one piece. "I'm so sorry." Louisa slowly stood up. "I hope I didn't tear your dress. I was going down and just grabbed. Your skirt was what I caught."

"You can't hurt this old thing," the woman replied. "I'm just glad you weren't hurt. Someone should move this wagon tongue. It's a menace." She looked around with a frown as if she was going to order the wagon tongue's movement post haste.

"I wasn't exactly looking where I was going," Louisa admitted. "It was my own fault."

"Oh well, no damage done." The woman ceased looking for the wagon's careless owner and turned to Louisa. "What's your name, child?"

"Louisa Lankford, ma'am."

"Is George Lankford your father?" The woman looked Louisa up and down.

"Yes, ma'am," Louisa said slowly. She couldn't tell at first if being her father's daughter was a good thing or not. But then a deep chuckle that seemed to start in the older woman's toes rolled over her.

"I've known George since he was just a boy blowing things up and setting things on fire when he was building his inventions." She shook her head. "What a lively thing he was. You must take after him."

Louisa grinned. "I guess I do, a little."

"Well, Louisa, why don't you carry my basket for a bit while I shop? We can talk."

Obediently Louisa took the huge basket from the woman, and they turned to walk among the stalls.

"Indeed, I was in touch with your father not that long ago. He made a donation to my Sunday school. Very generous he was." The woman stopped to look critically at some potatoes and onions.

"You must be Mrs. Jackson," Louisa said. "My father talked about you and your Sunday school for black children."

"Didn't I tell you my name yet? I am just so rude. Please forgive me, Louisa." She offered a coin to the farmer for some potatoes and a few onions. "Last year's crop," she said to Louisa in a low voice. "He's cleaning out his cellar before the new crop begins. But it will do for soup for the children."

"The children in your Sunday school?" Louisa held out the basket for the lumpy bundle of potatoes and onions.

"Yes, I try to feed the poor dears a little something each

53

week. At least some bread and soup." Mrs. Jackson stopped to examine some salted pork but quickly frowned and walked on. "They are often hungry, and a child just can't learn when his stomach is empty."

"What do you teach them?" Louisa asked. She remembered that her father had said that Mrs. Jackson was amazing. Louisa was beginning to understand why.

"We teach them to read and tell them Bible stories. Eventually we want them to be able to read the Bible for themselves. The black people are hungry for God's Word. A child who can read the Bible helps his whole family. Seems like it gives them some hope in this wicked old world." Mrs. Jackson stopped to finger a couple bolts of sturdy blue fabric that a peddler had among his wares. "Just too dear," she murmured to herself.

Louisa watched her. "Do they need clothes, too?"

"You have no idea, my dear. It just breaks my heart to see the rags they wear." Mrs. Jackson shook her head as if to clear it of discouraging thoughts. "But it's summer now, so they're warm again."

"Louisa." Mama was calling from a nearby stall.

"Coming," Louisa called back. "Mrs. Jackson, come and meet my mother."

"Land's sake, I know that sweet mother of yours, too. Here, let me take my basket." She took the big basket back on her arm and they walked over to Mama.

The two women greeted each other with pleasure and found much to talk about for a few minutes until a nearby church tolled the hour.

"Goodness, it's nine o'clock," Louisa's mother exclaimed.

"We'd better get this food home. It was a pleasure to see you again, Mrs. Jackson. Please let us know if we can help with your Sunday school in any way."

"You've already been most generous, Mrs. Lankford." Mrs. Jackson turned to Louisa. "Please come and see me some time, Louisa. I find you to be a most satisfactory young woman."

The older woman's words gave Louisa a warm feeling that lasted way beyond the walk home. It was nice to have someone besides her parents think she was a satisfactory person. It made yesterday's wax fruit episode seem less important.

But it didn't solve the problem. Did she get out the velvet and beeswax, or did she rebel? It was going to be a long summer.

CHAPTER 6
A Sorry State of Affairs

"Henry, are you ready?"

Henry could hear his sister Louisa's voice hollering up the stairs. Timothy must have arrived. He took one more swipe at his hair with a comb and went down the stairs at a run. He didn't want to keep his cousin waiting.

"Hi, Henry. Ready for the lecture?" At twenty-one, Timothy was tall and sturdy. Henry had long admired the older boy and was pleased to be invited to go somewhere with him.

"What kind of a lecture are you two attending?" Louisa asked.

"The speaker is James Birney, the publisher of the *Philanthropist*," Timothy replied.

"The abolitionist?" Louisa asked.

"The very one," Timothy replied.

"Sounds interesting," Louisa said.

"Maybe you can go next time," Henry said, "but we have to get going now."

He shoved the front door open and waited for Timothy to go out first. He wasn't about to take Louisa along.

"My friend Abe works for the printer who prints the *Philanthropist*," Henry said as he walked with Timothy the few blocks to the church where the lecture was to be held.

"Is that right? Then you must know lots about Mr. Birney already," Timothy said.

"I guess so." Henry grinned at his cousin, and as they walked, he told Timothy about the confrontation in front of the print shop.

"Sounds like Abe's Mr. Pugh did a good job of keeping the peace," Timothy said after hearing the story.

"They all got pretty stirred up," Henry said. "Seems like there's right and wrong in both sides." They were almost to the church steps. "Why can't they see that and be a little calmer about the whole thing?"

Timothy shook his head. "Slavery and its abolition is a real tricky subject right now. People just can't always stay calm. And maybe they shouldn't."

"What do you mean?" Henry asked as they went in the side door of the church.

Timothy stopped for a moment and looked at his cousin. "Slavery is a terrible thing, Henry. Getting rid of it is reason enough to take many actions that might seem rash under other circumstances. At least that's what I believe." Timothy turned and led the way into the church and sat at a place near the back of the room.

Henry followed his cousin. He knew that Timothy counted himself an abolitionist but had rather thought of that in the same way that someone might say that he was a Whig or a Republican. Those differences might lead to lots of arguments, but they never turned violent. It began to appear that abolition might inspire another kind of devotion.

After just a few minutes, James Birney walked to a podium at the front and began to speak. The large crowd of mostly men fell entirely silent as Mr. Birney's deep voice resounded through the room.

An hour passed before Henry even thought to wonder at the time. Mr. Birney told an interesting story. He talked of the slaves he had once owned, of his sorrow at that fact, and his joy in releasing them. He talked of giving up a lucrative legal practice in Alabama to return to Kentucky, the state of his birth. There he tried to establish an abolitionist newspaper but was forced to leave. So now he was in Cincinnati, and his newspaper was a reality. Henry listened intently. Here was a man who had sacrificed greatly for a cause that he believed in.

Mr. Birney continued with undiminished energy as he told stories of slavery's horrors and of his hopes for a better future for the blacks who were freemen as well as for the slaves to be freed. Henry glanced over once at Timothy. His cousin's face was shining as he leaned forward in his chair, eager not to miss a single word.

The lecture was well into its second hour when there were some scuffling noises and muffled voices behind Henry and Timothy. Henry ignored the commotion at first, but soon it became so loud that it was impossible to ignore. Mr. Birney continued to speak but the crowd began twisting in their seats to see what was happening. Henry finally turned to see that there were several men standing in the back who seemed to be discussing some issue vigorously among themselves.

At last the discussion commenced in full voice as one of the men yelled out, "Birney, we don't need the likes of you here in Cincinnati stirring up our citizens. Take yourself off to Boston or Philadelphia or some such place."

"We've told you before that we don't want all this foolishness about abolition," another man yelled. "You're just asking for trouble."

The crowd murmured, but no one spoke up. Henry looked back up at the pulpit. James Birney appeared not at all upset by the interruption. In fact, his face was calm and perhaps resolute. He waited a few moments before speaking again. "Friends, please come up here to the front. I would be more than happy to discuss this issue with you. It is always helpful to air our differences. I'm sure these kind people would delight in the chance to share in a debate."

"That we would," someone yelled from the audience. "If you want to interrupt our lecture, then provide us with some other avenue for learning."

"Birney," a tall skinny man who was doing most of the

talking said, "you just don't understand. We don't want to discuss and debate this abolition nonsense. There's nothing to talk about. Talking just gets people all excited over nothing."

"Our nation was founded on the doctrine of free speech, sir," said Birney. "It's our duty to discuss the issues that divide us." He walked to the edge of the raised platform area. "And believe me, friends, when I say that slavery will divide us."

"It's you and your fanatic associates who are making the division," said the skinny man. "The blacks, slave and free, would be better off if you stopped agitating the situation."

At this, several members of the crowd jumped up and began to yell at the man. Before long there were various groups engaged in intense argument with the men at the back and among themselves.

"Looks like this is the end of this lecture," Timothy said. "We'd better go."

"Do we have to leave?" Henry asked.

"I don't think your parents would appreciate it if I let you get caught in the midst of a full-fledged brawl," Timothy said.

"Do you think that will happen?" Henry stopped where he was in the aisle. A brawl was something he hadn't witnessed before and wouldn't mind seeing.

Timothy laughed softly. "I don't know, but we're not going to find out, either, you bloodthirsty creature."

In a few minutes the cousins were on their way down the street toward Henry's house. It was almost nine o'clock, so the streets were quiet—quiet enough for Henry to think as he walked. He thought about slavery in a different way than ever before. He had been brought up to believe that slavery was wrong, and of course he never intended to own slaves, but Mr. Birney had made him wonder if that was enough. Mr. Birney said that no Christian should rest until slavery was eliminated.

"Penny for your thoughts," Timothy said.

Henry looked over at his cousin. "They're not worth that much I guess." He hesitated a moment and then asked, "Do you think Mr. Birney was right about a Christian's responsibility to do away with slavery?"

"Yes, I do," Timothy replied. "The Bible says that we are all cast in God's image and equal in his sight. I think that means black and white and red and any other color of skin that we haven't seen before. If we believe that, then we have to do whatever it takes to make our everyday life match the biblical example."

"I see what you're saying, although I can't say that I've ever looked at it quite that way," Henry said. "But I will."

"Now that doesn't mean that I think everyone is cut out to travel and lecture like Mr. Birney or publish a newspaper," Timothy said as they started to cross a street. "God gives us all certain talents. We just have to figure out the right way to use those talents. I want to go back east to study law as soon as I can save a little more money. What about you?"

"Oh, I'm going to be a doctor," Henry answered automatically. "I've wanted to be a doctor ever since the cholera epidemic." He stopped short as he remembered something else about the cholera epidemic of four years ago.

"The epidemic that killed my father," Timothy stated bluntly. "I wasn't even here when he died. I was away at my grandpa's."

61

"I remember," Henry said.

"Well, it's good that you should be a doctor, Henry. Maybe your talents can help prevent another epidemic."

Henry started to speak, but sounds of scuffling and muffled shouts distracted him. "What's that?"

Timothy stopped and listened. "I'm not sure. It sounds like it might be down and around the corner. Want to take a peek?"

"Can we?" Henry asked. The sounds were getting louder.

"Just a peek. We don't want to get ourselves beat up unless it's absolutely necessary."

"For the common good," Henry hissed as they stepped quickly through the shadows.

Timothy laughed softly. "The only reason to get beat up."

Their good humor faded as they rounded the street corner and saw what was going on. The light from an open door shone into the street, illuminating four men who stood over a black man cowering on the limestone-paved street. The block of mostly shops was deserted at this time of night unless the owners lived above the shops. Henry didn't see anyone else about.

"We told you not to go down this street no more," a voice yelled.

"Can't have the likes of you walking anywhere you please," another voice spoke in the dark.

"I was a-going for the doctor." The black man's voice was muffled but clear.

There was loud laughter among the white men. Henry started to press forward at this, but Timothy put his hand out and grabbed Henry's arm.

"Well now, isn't that a whopper," one of the men yelled. "As if any doctor would go to Little Africa."

"It would be a sorry state of affairs indeed if our white doctors started traipsing over there." There was more loud laughter.

"Can't we do something?" Henry asked Timothy urgently. The pair had stopped by the side of a cabinetmaker's shop. "Can't we call the watch or something?"

"The watch won't do anything to help a black man," Timothy said, "and we're very much outnumbered." He looked around. "It will have to be in the nature of a distraction."

Just then Henry heard a different sound. He peered through the darkness. One of the men was kicking the black man, who grunted with each blow but didn't cry out. Henry grabbed Timothy. "We've got to do something now!"

"Come here," Timothy whispered and pulled Henry into the alley next to the cabinetmaker's shop. "Help me," Timothy said as he quickly stacked some discarded crates that were in the alley.

Henry followed suit, and soon they had a precarious tower several feet high. Then Timothy scrounged on the ground and came up with a handful of small rocks.

"When I say so, give the tower a big shove toward the street and take off running as fast as you can down the alley," Timothy instructed. He sneaked back to the street.

Henry listened. The beating seemed to have stopped or at least paused. The men were talking more quietly now. He watched as Timothy also listened and then threw the rocks out into the street, where they hit the limestone paving with a rattling sound.

"What was that?" one of the men said. "Who's there?"

Timothy threw more rocks and motioned for Henry to topple the tower. Henry gave the crates a mighty shove and ran as swiftly as his legs could take him down the alley. The crates tumbled with a loud crash, but Henry didn't look back. He hoped that Timothy was right behind him. He heard shouts but still he kept running.

At last he slowed and stopped by the side of a church on the street that the alley had led to. He looked back and saw a figure running toward him. It was Timothy. Henry realized that they were pretty visible in the dark with their white shirts. Timothy pulled Henry into the shadows, where they leaned, panting, against the side of the building.

"Did he get away?" Henry whispered.

"I'm not sure," Timothy said. "They all ran toward the noise at first. Probably he bolted when they did that."

"Can't we go check?" Henry wanted to know firsthand that the black man had escaped.

"No, it's not safe," Timothy answered in a low voice. "They won't hesitate to call the watch on us. No, we'll just have to trust that God gave that man an extra measure of strength." He peeked out of their hiding place. "Let's go. It's getting late. We'll have to take the long way home, so we'd better hurry."

Henry reluctantly followed his cousin. They walked in silence for several blocks.

Timothy finally spoke. "That's why I want to be a lawyer."

"What do you mean?"

"Those men could have had that man arrested, even though all he was doing was walking through the streets."

"Was he a slave?" Henry asked.

"No, he was as free as you and I, but black people have no legal rights."

"And you want to help them," Henry said.

"Yes, more than anything," Timothy said. "If a man is under the authority of the law, then he should also have the protection of that law."

They were at Henry's front porch now.

"I better get on home myself," Timothy said. "Tell your parents what happened, Henry. I hope they won't be upset. Most lectures I go to are downright boring."

"Not this one," Henry said and waved to his cousin, who sprinted down the walk and into the dark.

No, boring was not the word for this evening. He had lots of new ideas to think about. He just hoped he could turn his brain off long enough to get some sleep.

CHAPTER 7

The Society

Louisa was shocked when she heard Henry's story the next morning at breakfast. "Do you think that man was hurt very badly?" she asked as she ate her oatmeal.

"I'm not sure," Henry said. "Maybe not. I only saw them kick him once or twice."

"I wonder why he was going for a doctor?" Louisa frowned as she scraped the last of her breakfast from the bowl. "He must have been desperate or he wouldn't have risked going through that neighborhood."

"I know, and I kept thinking about that in the night," Henry said. "Maybe I could have helped if we had been able to get to the man."

"You did all you could to help," his mother said firmly.

"Maybe more than you should, for safety's sake at least." She poured coffee into her husband's cup.

"Your mother's right," Henry's father said. "You and Timothy did all that could have been done under the circumstances. And it was pretty quick thinking at that." He sipped at his fresh coffee. "I'd like to have seen those men's faces when they came up empty-handed, for I'm sure that the black man was able to get away. But you know what? I think we should stop right now and pray for that man and his family and for the men who were attacking him."

The family bowed their heads while Papa offered prayers for all involved in what he called "the shameful episode last evening." Louisa knew that her father always prayed for enemies, but sometimes it was hard to understand why—and this was one of those times.

Louisa was helping her mother clear the breakfast dishes when she had an idea. She could see Henry stacking wood out in the back. "Mama, we could use some eggs," she said. "Why don't I go to the market for you?"

"That's a good idea," Mama said as she dropped spoons into a dishpan of soapy water. "I have so much to do this morning, and I want Anna to do some extra baking."

"I'll ask Henry to go with me, I think, if he doesn't have to work for Papa or Dr. Drake."

"That's an even better idea," her mother said. "Take some coins from the jar over there."

Louisa took a couple coins, grabbed her bonnet off the hook in the entryway, and ran down the back steps. "Henry!"

Henry looked up from his work. "What is it?"

"Come with me to the market, and we'll see if we can

find Mrs. Jackson. She might know something about that man from last night."

"Mrs. Jackson? Who's she? Oh, wait, now I remember. She's the lady with the black Sunday school," Henry said. He kept stacking the wood that had been delivered the previous day.

"That's right, and I bet she knows everything that goes on down there in the black section of town."

Henry thought for a moment. "You might be right, and what can it hurt to ask? Great idea. Let's go." He dusted off his hands. "I need to be at Dr. Drake's in an hour. He just got back from a spell of teaching in Pittsburgh, so there will be lots to do."

Louisa led the way. It wasn't often that she had an idea that her older brother hadn't had first. She liked the feeling.

Rachel and Calvin weren't in their usual spot at the market, so Louisa carefully selected two dozen eggs from another farmer's supply and paid for them. All the while she kept her eyes open for Mrs. Jackson.

"Let's walk around a little bit," Louisa said. "She could be anywhere among these stalls and carts."

Henry took the basket, and they threaded their way through the early morning crowd. It was still cool, and the smells of fresh produce mingled with that of bakery goods. Louisa scanned the shoppers for Mrs. Jackson's stout figure. There was lots to see, but no Mrs. Jackson.

"Look," Henry said and pointed to a huddle of people to their left.

"What?"

There was a ripple of laughter from the group.

"I think it's a trained monkey," Henry said and stretched his head high so he could see better. "Yes, that's it. He's doing tricks."

"Oh, let's watch," Louisa said. She skirted the group to find a place where she could see through the arms and legs of shoppers shoved close to see the show.

"Over here," Henry said and pointed to a box she could stand on.

Once on the box, Louisa could see the monkey. He was scruffy looking but jumped around doing tricks at his master's command. The crowd laughed and clapped at each trick, and a few tossed coins into a cup held by the monkey's equally shabby owner.

"Well, if it isn't Louisa," a woman's voice said from nearby. "And about to take another tumble if I'm any judge."

Louisa twisted to see who was talking and indeed started to fall off her box. Henry grabbed her arm, and instead of landing in a heap on the ground, she jumped somewhat gracefully down.

"Mrs. Jackson! You're just the person we were looking for. That is we were looking for you before the monkey started performing." Louisa walked over to the woman's side. "This is my brother, Henry."

Introductions made, Louisa continued, "We wanted to ask you about something." Louisa took Mrs. Jackson's hand and pulled her a little ways from the group still watching the monkey's antics. She explained their hope that Mrs. Jackson would know something about the events of the previous night. Mrs. Jackson listened in silence as Henry told what had happened in the street.

When he finished, she sighed deeply. "I haven't heard about this yet, but I probably will. Usually they come to me if they need a doctor, and I take care of it. I was gone last evening helping with the birthing of a baby, so maybe he didn't think it could wait."

"Does this happen very often?" Louisa asked.

"All the time, I'm afraid," Mrs. Jackson said. "But this time it could have been much worse if not for Henry and Timothy. I thank you, young man. I'll find out more and send a message to you."

"Thank you," Henry said. "I would like to be sure that the man isn't hurt."

There was a final burst of applause for the monkey, who then scrambled on his master's shoulder as the crowd moved away. Louisa sidestepped a little girl who raced by. "Are you shopping for your Sunday school again?"

"That I am, my dear, and I found some lovely bargains. The good Lord does provide. A farmer gave me a nice fat old hen for a ridiculously low price, so I'm planning a real treat for the children, dumplings in a nice rich broth. Makes my mouth water." She laughed at her good fortune.

Louisa laughed, too. Mrs. Jackson made a person want to laugh at the least little things, even dumplings.

"Speaking of food," Henry said, "we'd better get these eggs home, Louisa."

They took their leave, and Mrs. Jackson promised again to send them a message as soon as she found out anything about the man who'd been attacked. They hurried on home, chattering as they went about Mrs. Jackson and her Sunday school. Once home, Henry went off to Dr. Drake's, and Louisa tied on

70

a big apron to help Anna with the baking.

That afternoon found Louisa walking over to Martha's once more. According to her friend, the girls were going to organize the club while they stitched on their needlework. Louisa wasn't sure what kind of organizing they needed to do, but she was still hopeful that they could do something more important than make silly wax fruit. Painting or drawing might be interesting, but on velvet? That sounded just as silly as fruit she couldn't eat. But it was something to do until something better came along.

She thought about Mrs. Jackson as she walked. In spite of the problems she had to deal with, the woman seemed happy. She was certainly cheerful. Louisa wondered about the children that Mrs. Jackson tried to teach and provide for. They no doubt concentrated on survival most of the time. It was a sobering thought when she compared their lives to her own. It made this wax fruit business just that much more frustrating. What a waste of time!

All of her friends were gathered in their usual arrangement around Julia when Louisa arrived. They talked noisily as they stitched away at samplers or made lace. Louisa seated herself and pulled out a large bundle of cloth from her new needlework bag. She never had found the lost one. She threaded her needle and set to work.

"What are you stitching, Louisa dear?" Julia drawled. "It's quite large." She held up her own bit of lace to the light and surveyed it critically.

"Oh, I'm mending a sheet," Louisa answered. She shifted the lump of cloth on her lap, and it flopped to the floor around her feet.

"A sheet?" Julia giggled and tossed her curls. "You're such a character, Louisa."

Louisa clenched her teeth but raised her head to bestow a huge smile on Julia. "I just wanted to be doing something useful." She bent back over the sheet. Her mother would be shocked if she knew that Louisa had pulled the old sheet out of the mending basket and stuffed it into her needlework bag. It was a small protest, but she felt a little better.

"Let's get started on organizing our self-improvement society, girls," Julia said. "I believe we should elect officers first thing."

"Officers? Why?" Louisa spoke up without thinking.

Julia gave her a pitying look. "All organizations have officers. Ours should be no exception."

Addie and Sally were nodding in agreement.

"That sounds right," Miranda said.

"I suppose it can't hurt," Martha added. Louisa gave her friend a disgusted look, but Martha just shrugged her shoulders.

"I nominate Julia for president," Addie said.

"Oh, yes," Sally agreed. "The society was her idea. She should be president."

"I'm flattered, to be sure," Julia said sweetly, "but we must observe the conventions and elect our officers."

Louisa let her thoughts drift while the others took on the task of electing Julia. Mrs. Jackson just kept coming back to her mind. She was sure that that woman didn't spend time sitting around stitching lace. Any stitching she did would be likely to produce something more substantial. Which is what Louisa would like to be doing.

She held the sheet up to look for another rip to mend. This old sheet would make two or three shirts or simple shift dresses for the Sunday school children. Louisa remembered that Mrs. Jackson had been looking at material for clothing but had found it too expensive. Now that Louisa thought about it, there were a couple bolts of muslin in the linen cupboard at home. They were probably intended for sheets.

Louisa frowned at the sheet in her lap. Maybe she could sew some shirts and shifts from that material for the children. She hadn't actually ever done that kind of sewing, because her mother usually employed a seamstress to make their clothing a couple times a year. But how hard could it be?

"Louisa! Louisa! You're daydreaming." Martha's voice interrupted her thoughts.

Louisa brought herself back to the present. The others were looking expectantly at her. "What?"

"We've just elected you sergeant-at-arms," Julia said. "Will you accept?"

"Sergeant-at-arms? Me?" Louisa said and dropped her sheet. "I guess. What do I do?"

They all looked at Julia, who laughed and shook her curls again. "Why, silly, you keep the order at the meetings."

"Oh, I see. I think," Louisa said. "You mean I straighten out any member who gets unruly."

"Technically, yes," Julia replied, "but it's really more of an honorary position."

Louisa had a fleeting urge to straighten out the new president, but then remembered her train of thought before being interrupted. "Oh, fine. I'll do it, but I have another idea for the club." Maybe she could convince them to sew for Mrs. Jackson's children.

"Indeed," Julia said formally. "We'll consider it, I'm sure, in the proper order. Now let's get down to the business at hand. We should make a list of supplies for our proposed projects and each bring something to our next meeting."

"My idea has to do with our projects," Louisa persisted.

"Oh, very well," Julia said with a touch of irritation. "What is it?"

Quickly Louisa outlined her idea for sewing shirts and shifts for the children at Mrs. Jackson's Sunday school. "We could still have a club or society. It would just be for a different purpose. More of a benevolent society, I suppose you might say. Actually," she conceded, "it could be a branch of the self-improvement society. We could still do the other things. When we had time, that is."

Louisa paused to glance at the others for their reactions. Martha was smiling, but Julia's normally smooth brow was creased in a frown. She looked like a summer thunderstorm about to break. Miranda, Addie, and Sally just looked from Louisa to Julia and back again.

"We've been through this before, Louisa." Julia sat up straighter. "Yours is an admirable plan, I'm sure, but we don't want to sew shirts." She shook her head slightly. "Especially not for slaves and their kind." Although Julia's last words were said under her breath, Louisa clearly heard them.

"Is that so?" Louisa jumped up. It was one thing to disagree, but quite another to be rude.

"It does sound like a good idea," Martha put in. "Surely we'll have time to do some charity work, too, Julia." Martha quietly placed a hand on Louisa's arm and stared at Julia.

Julia hesitated. At last she made a slight grimace and spoke. "Oh, I suppose there might be time. We'll just have to see." She turned and began to talk to Addie about types of velvet.

Martha smiled at Louisa. "Not exactly a victory," she said in a low voice, "but it was close. It's a great idea, Louisa. We'll get it done somehow."

"Not if she has anything to do with it." Louisa nodded her head in Julia's direction.

"She doesn't know everything," Martha said.

"That's for sure," Louisa agreed, and they both laughed.

CHAPTER 8
So Much for Free Speech

"Louisa, where are you?" Henry yelled as he went in the front door of his house and walked quickly down the hallway toward the kitchen.

"Don't yell in the house, Henry," his mother said from the kitchen table where she was shelling peas. "Your sister is out on the back porch."

"Sorry," Henry said with a grin and continued on his way.

"What is it?" Louisa pushed open the back door. "Is something wrong?"

"No," he replied, "it's the opposite."

"So tell me." Louisa took the broom she had been using on the steps and put it back in the corner.

"Mrs. Jackson sent a message to us at the shipyard. Papa told me as soon as I got there after making my river observations."

"What was the message?" Louisa asked.

"She said that the man was named Elijah, and he was fine." Henry took the dipper and got a drink of water from the water pail. "He was only bruised—and not badly at that. I guess those men must not have been kicking him as hard as it sounded. The woman who needed the doctor is better, too."

Henry felt a great sense of relief to know that the man wasn't seriously hurt. The injustice of the beating was bad enough, but it was even worse in his mind to go off and leave an injured man to his fate.

"They must have been weaklings, or maybe they really didn't want to hurt him," Louisa said.

"Maybe," Henry said doubtfully, "but it didn't seem that way Tuesday night."

"At least he's not hurt too much, and he's not in jail," Louisa said.

"I guess I should be satisfied, but somehow it doesn't seem like enough." Henry took another drink of water. "I hadn't realized that there was so much hatred toward the black people in our city. I guess I just didn't think about it."

"I know what you mean. Meeting Julia Garnett has been an interesting experience." Louisa assumed a pose and flipped back her hair in imitation of the Georgia girl. "La, child, just send a darkie after it," she drawled as she fluttered her eyelids.

Henry laughed. "Her brother, Walter, isn't much better." He dropped the dipper with a plop. "I've got to get to Dr. Drake's. See you later." He was off down the hall and out the door. It wouldn't do to be late. The doctor was taking him along to visit hospital patients today, which was a treat in Henry's eyes.

Several hours later he was on his way home when he saw a placard in front of a meeting hall. It caught his attention because at the top in big letters it said, ATTENTION: YOUNG MEN—AGES TWELVE TO TWENTY.

He stopped to read the rest of the sign. It advertised a meeting of the American Colonization Society to be held in the hall on Saturday evening. Evidently the meeting was for young men. The placard further stated that the meeting was for the purpose of discussion and debate on the subject of colonization of the blacks.

Henry studied the sign for a minute and then walked on. He had heard of the American Colonization Society, but that was about all. Maybe it was time to find out more, and if so, then this meeting was the perfect opportunity.

Who could he get to go with him? He knew that Timothy was leaving on a trip for Pittsburgh before the weekend. Maybe Raleigh and Abe could be persuaded to go to the meeting. He'd ask them that evening.

As it turned out, Abe couldn't go because he was traveling to visit his family on Saturday and Sunday, but Raleigh was enthusiastic. They set a time to meet Saturday evening.

"I wish I could go," Louisa said Saturday when Henry was leaving.

Henry grabbed his cap on the way out the door. "I

wouldn't mind, but the sign said the meeting was for young men. Sorry."

"Girls never get to do anything," she said.

"Oh, now, I wouldn't say that," he said. "You get to make wax fruit and paint—on velvet!"

The only thing close at hand was a towel, so Louisa threw that at her brother. "You're impossible."

Henry laughed as the towel dropped to the floor. "You'll get your chance someday." He ducked out the door to escape more of his sister's wrath. It was hard to resist teasing her sometimes, even though he understood her feelings.

When he reached the hall fifteen minutes later, there was no sign of Raleigh out in front where they were supposed to meet. There were quite a few boys and young men filing into the building and a few older men. The older men must be the organizers, he decided. The number of new arrivals had slowed down to a trickle, and still there was no sign of Raleigh. The clock in the church tower down the street was striking seven o'clock when Raleigh appeared, panting, with Walter in tow.

"I thought you weren't coming," Henry said and raised his eyebrows at Raleigh while Walter leaned against the door trying to get his breath back.

Raleigh rolled his eyes. "Sorry, we were delayed. Walter stopped by and decided to come with me."

Walter adjusted his shirt front. "I thought this meeting might be interesting. The American Colonization Society is banned in Georgia. I think it's another bunch of nuts like the abolitionists, but I'd like to see for myself."

"That's fine," Henry said. "Come on. Let's hurry so we

79

can find a place to sit."

The meeting was just starting as the boys entered. A young man of nineteen or twenty stood behind a podium at the front. "We'll start this meeting with a welcome from John Edgeway. Mr. Edgeway is the president of the Cincinnati Men's Branch of the American Colonization Society."

Henry, Raleigh, and Walter sat down as quietly as possible in chairs near the back. Mr. Edgeway droned on for several minutes about the noble purpose of the organization and the critical need for action and hence an even more critical need for funds.

Raleigh jabbed Henry in the side and whispered, "He's after money."

Henry grinned and nodded. He leaned back a little in his chair. So far he hadn't heard a thing that helped him know what the Colonization Society specifically stood for. Of course he knew that it had to do with sending black people to Africa, but why and how?

Finally Mr. Edgeway asked if there were any questions. Perhaps this would lead to the discussion and debate promised on the placard announcing the meeting. Henry hoped so. At first it looked like he was going to have to ask the first question if it was going to get asked. Just as Henry was mentally phrasing a question, a skinny, freckled-faced young man spoke up. "What is it exactly that the society wants to do?"

"Excellent question, lad. Gets right to the heart of the matter. Never assume anything," said Mr. Edgeway.

Henry sat up a little taller so he could be sure to hear what was said. He noticed that Walter was listening intently, too.

Probably just wanted more reason to call the colonizationists nuts.

"The society has as its heartfelt goal to transport Christian blacks to Africa, where they will be a strong influence in civilizing that great dark continent." Mr. Edgeway hooked his thumbs in his waistcoat and walked back and forth in front of the podium while he spoke. "In Africa, their native home, the black people will find a more congenial atmosphere for the development of their latent talents."

"What's he talking about?" Raleigh whispered.

"I told you they were crazy," Walter said.

"Shh, just listen for a minute," Henry said. He frowned in concentration.

"But weren't most of the black people around now born in America?" It was the freckled young man again. "They've never even been to Africa. Why would they want to go there?"

"It is the home of their ancestors, and the one place on this earth where they can fulfill their destiny," Mr. Edgeway replied.

Henry found that line of thought less than direct, but perhaps he had misunderstood. Time to ask his own questions. He stood and asked, "Is this effort to be directed toward the free blacks or only slaves?"

"Our first objective is the free blacks," Mr. Edgeway answered. "A return to his homeland would give the free black real freedom as opposed to the nominal existence he now has."

"And the slaves?"

"We advocate the gradual emancipation of slaves as

rapidly as is practical. They would go then to join the other blacks already comfortably settled in their new colonies in Africa."

Henry heard a snort from Walter, who evidently was finding something with which to disagree. It wasn't in Henry's plan to agree with Walter, but at this point he could see some holes in the colonization plan himself.

"What if they don't want to go?" someone called out from the audience.

"Are you gonna make them go?" another voice yelled.

"We must consider this calmly, my friends," Mr. Edgeway said. His voice had grown tighter. "We feel absolutely certain that any prudent black man or woman would appreciate the opportunity to take part in this great experiment."

"You just want to ship them off so they won't want to live in your neighborhoods." It was a new voice from the back of the room. The owner of the voice was a man Henry recognized from the abolition lecture.

Mr. Edgeway sputtered his indignation, "Not at all. We have only their best interests in mind." The audience stirred as they turned to see who was talking in the back.

"I suggest that you wish to rid our country of what you see as an undesirable element," the man in the back said. "Ship them back to Africa so we can forget what hideous injustices we have served on these people."

Henry suddenly realized that he was still standing. Quickly he sat down. What would happen now?

One of the other older men who had accompanied Mr. Edgeway jumped up. "This type of discussion is totally inappropriate. We'll thank you to leave right now, sir."

There was scattered grumbling from the audience—some in agreement and some not from what Henry could hear. Why couldn't they just sit down and talk? He'd like to hear what the other man had to say. Surely Mr. Edgeway would want to prove his point fairly.

"I bear no ill will toward Mr. Edgeway, sir," the man in the back spoke again. "I would welcome the opportunity to discuss this issue. Perhaps I can be convinced of the society's good intentions." This last was said with a smile, and several in the crowd chuckled.

Henry slowly rose again. "Please, sir, let us hear from them both," he said. His words came in a gap in the muttering and rumblings of the audience and sounded terribly loud to his own ears.

It was as if his words had ignited the listening crowd. Everyone began to talk at once and loudly. Some called for an end to the talk and others shouted to let the gentlemen get on with a debate. Mr. Edgeway had been shifted away from the podium. Three other men, including the one who had spoken earlier, stood in a line in front of the podium.

One of them gave Henry an angry look. "Sit down, son. You're being impertinent. This meeting wasn't intended to be a public debate."

Henry hesitated, but his parents' teaching about respect for his elders finally made him sit down. But sitting down didn't put a stop to his surging anger. Impertinent, indeed! He had never been called that before, or at least not for a long time. How could it be impertinent to want to talk about something so important?

It was obvious that the meeting was at an end. In a few

minutes the three boys were on their way home. Henry was still angry. He had always been encouraged to have his say. That was how it was done in his family. Be polite, but be heard.

"I wasn't expecting that," Raleigh said.

"I told you they were all nuts," Walter said. "Slaves can never just be turned loose. They can't provide for themselves. Besides, we need our slaves, and we paid for them fair and square."

"You can't just buy and sell people," Henry said and threw up his hands. "They're not cattle."

"Sure you can. It's legal." Walter gave Henry a superior smile. "Besides, I've said it before, and I'll say it again. Blacks aren't people. Not in the way you mean at least."

"Aggh!" Henry spouted in frustration. He gave Walter the most disgusted look he could manage and stomped off down the street, leaving the other two in his wake. For once, Henry had lost his taste for a good disagreement.

CHAPTER 9
Martha Prevails

"I knew I should have gone with you," Louisa said at breakfast the next morning after Henry told his story. "Exciting stuff always happens to you."

"No, it doesn't. My days are just as boring as yours."

Louisa made a face at her brother.

"Well, maybe not quite as boring as yours," Henry admitted. "That would have to be pretty dull."

"You probably go out looking for ways to stir things up," Louisa announced as she took a last drink of milk.

"I don't, but it just happens lately."

"Children! Quit your teasing," Mama said as she brought

85

some more bread to the table. "This is the Sabbath. You two would be better served to think about your roles as Christians. Now finish your breakfast and get ready for services."

Louisa turned her attention to one more piece of bread and butter. When she glanced at her brother, he grinned at her. She couldn't help grinning back. She knew he didn't actually go looking for trouble, but that didn't stop her from feeling jealous.

Just then their father called from the front porch that he had brought the carriage around from the nearby stable. As soon as they picked up Miss Emma, they would be off to church.

Sunday service was long, but Louisa didn't usually mind too much. She listened to the Reverend McCall for as long as she could because her parents expected it. Sometimes she was surprised at all she learned. When her brain just couldn't concentrate anymore on the preacher's big words, she let herself daydream. Whether God minded that or not, she wasn't sure, but she tended to think He understood.

It was hot in the church during the summer, and this day was no exception. Louisa settled herself and looked around as much as she dared. Her mother frowned if Louisa turned around in the pew, so she had to confine most of her looking to the front. Martha was there with her family, and Addie with her family. Julia's Aunt Cynthia was sitting in her usual place.

Julia wasn't there, although Walter sat beside his aunt. Louisa wondered where the visitor from Georgia was. Julia had come with her aunt on other Sundays decked out in all her finery. Privately Louisa thought that was the reason Julia came to church—to show off her clothes.

"Christ is all, and is in all!" The preacher boomed out his text, and Louisa jumped. This came after some hymn singing and a long prayer. The Reverend McCall certainly knew how to get a person's attention, she had to admit.

"Ephesians 3:11 tells us all we need to know," he continued in a quieter voice. "It matters not whether we are Greek or Jew, a barbarian, a Scythian, or even slave or free. Christ is in each of us."

Louisa didn't know any barbarians or Scythians and she didn't think she knew any Greeks or Jews, but she knew about slaves. Was the Reverend McCall speaking to his congregation about slaves? She had often wondered if a preacher had a list of sermons or maybe a book that told him what to preach and when. It seemed too much of a coincidence for him to have happened onto a sermon about problems in Cincinnati right now.

She wished she dared ask her father, but of course that was out of the question. He sat quietly beside her with his eyes focused on the preacher.

Louisa turned her attention back to the Reverend McCall's words. Now he was talking about Ephesians 3:12.

"Clothe yourself with compassion, kindness, humility, gentleness, and patience. God expects that we follow His rules for holy living in all of our dealings with other people," the Reverend McCall said. "Not just when we like the other people or just when we agree with them, but all the time."

Louisa frowned as an image of Julia popped into her mind. It felt like a little barb pricking her. The Reverend

McCall was talking about people like Julia, too, not just blacks or barbarians or Scythians. Julia, who was annoying and spoiled and thought slavery was a good idea. Louisa couldn't suppress a sigh as this thought sunk in. Sometimes she wished being a Christian was still the same as when she was younger. Then all she really had to do was obey her parents, which wasn't too hard because her parents were usually fair.

Now that she was older, she was supposed to think for herself. She just hoped God understood how much harder that was. Patience with Julia—now that was a task for Hercules or someone else with more strength than she had. She sat quietly, trying to listen to the preacher but mostly hearing the bees buzzing in the honeysuckle bush outside the window.

At last the service was over. "You're awfully quiet, Cricket," Louisa's father said. They had delivered Miss Emma to her door and left the carriage and horse at the stable and were now walking the short distance home. Louisa smiled at his use of the nickname that he had given her as a baby when he said she was always jumping around.

"Just thinking," she said. "Why do some people who go to church still own slaves or at least not think that blacks are the equals of whites?" She voiced the question that had been on her mind for days.

"Ah, the tough questions for a lovely June afternoon," her father said with a smile. "You're wise to ask that question, but I'm not sure if I'm wise enough to answer it." He looked up at the blue sky as if searching for an answer written there.

"Many people who own slaves, be they churchgoers or not, are antislavery," he said.

"But how is that possible?" Louisa burst out.

"Let me finish. For them the question has become how to free their slaves rather than how to keep them. There is much disagreement about what is the most humane and practical way to free the slaves. And even more disagreement about what to do with them once they are free."

"The colonizationists and the abolitionists are both anti-slavery," Henry put in, "but they sure don't agree on how to get rid of it."

"You're right, Son, and as you have seen, sometimes the differences in opinion can lead to outright quarreling."

"But what about people like Julia and Walter?" Louisa asked. "They sure aren't antislavery." Every time she thought about how Julia used the word darkie, it made her angry.

"They sure aren't," Henry said. "In fact, Walter said that they needed their slaves, that they were bought and paid for."

Papa shook his head. "The Garnett youngsters are from Georgia, as you know, and Georgia is in the Deep South. They are reflecting their background just as you would if you traveled to Georgia. Slavery is very entrenched in the Deep South. People who live there can't see any future without it."

"But surely that doesn't make it right," Louisa said.

"No, not at all, but it does help us to understand their attitudes. Only by first understanding can we hope to help them change their minds about slavery, or at least help them adjust to what will surely happen some day." Papa took

Mama's arm to guide her around a branch that had fallen on the sidewalk.

"What will happen?" Louisa asked, although she wasn't sure she wanted to know.

Her father's face was grave. "Slavery will be abolished, and I fear our whole nation may suffer from the consequences of that action. We must pray long and often for wisdom for our leaders. A prayer for patience to deal with people like Walter and Julia couldn't hurt, either," he added with a smile.

Louisa fell silent for the rest of the walk home. She had much to think about.

It was barely ten o'clock the next morning when Martha appeared at the Lankfords' house. Louisa had just finished helping Anna hang the weekly laundry on lines across the back yard when she heard Martha's voice next to her.

"Guess what?"

Louisa laughed. "You've been invited to meet the president?"

"No, silly." She giggled. "I talked to Addie and Sally and Miranda, and we all want to help you with sewing for Mrs. Jackson's Sunday school children."

"What about Julia and the self-improvement society?"

"We'll still do that, but there's time for both." Martha folded her hands in front of her. "Let's face it. None of us is terribly busy this summer. If Julia wants to help with the sewing, she can. Otherwise, we'll do it without her."

"She'll be aggravated," Louisa warned as she stacked the empty baskets that had held the wet clothes.

"Probably, but it doesn't hurt that she has the summer

complaint and won't be out and about for a few days."

"That's why she wasn't at church. Is she very sick?" Louisa tried not to show her relief that Julia was out of circulation for the near future.

"No, not at all. She'll be fine, but her Aunt Cynthia told my mother that Julia is a terrible patient. One minute she acts like she's dying, and the next she's demanding this and that." Martha held the back door open for Louisa to come through with her load of baskets.

Louisa laughed. "Now why am I not surprised to hear that? But I'm glad she's not really sick." Louisa had resolved to try to understand Julia, but it might be more easily accomplished at a distance, at least for a few days.

"Well, what are we waiting for?" Martha asked. "Let's take a look at that material you mentioned. My mother said she'd trace some patterns for us, and Miranda said there are tons of buttons at her house, and thread, too." The girls went arm-in-arm to enlist Louisa's mother to help with their cause.

The next week was a busy one. Making shirts and shifts turned out to be a lot harder than it looked. Even all the help their mothers gave them didn't keep the girls from making lots of mistakes. But finally they had first one shirt and then two and then a couple of shifts done.

One hot afternoon toward the end of June, they gathered on Addie's big front porch to stitch and try to catch any breeze that might drift by. They dragged some stools and chairs outside to sit on.

"I never knew that it would be so much harder to sew real

clothes than to make lace and fancy piecework," Martha confessed.

"I have a lot more sympathy for the seamstress who has to sew our clothes." Louisa held up a shirt to survey the button-hole she had just finished. "These shirts are pretty simple, and the shifts even more so. Just think how long it takes for us to do just one."

"We're just plain slow," Miranda said and wiped some sweat from her nose.

"And hot!" Sally added.

"I declare, girls. What are you up to?" A familiar south-ern drawl drifted over them.

"Julia!" They all jumped up and went to greet her as she climbed the porch steps like royalty.

"Are you better?"

"You were sick a long time!"

"Were you just bored to tears?"

They led her to a chair and made her sit down. "Now tell us all about it," Miranda said.

Julia fluttered a fan she was carrying. "It was dreadful, but I'm better now. I have such a delicate constitution, you know. It just took days and days before I dared to get out of bed."

Louisa looked at Martha, who rolled her eyes, but the other girls uttered sympathetic noises.

They did get back to sewing after everything had been talked over and the sewing was explained to Julia with many reassurances as to their unswerving intention to con-tinue with the self-improvement society.

Louisa was pleasantly surprised when Julia seemed to

take the project in stride. She appeared to be not the least upset that they had undertaken something that she had dismissed only a couple weeks earlier. Louisa felt guilty for thinking that Julia would be aggravated. Her guilt subsided a bit when Julia begged off from helping the others sew. She vowed that she was still too weak from her illness. Louisa smiled and bent to her sewing. Some things stayed the same.

While Louisa and her friends had been sewing shirts and shifts, Henry had been working at the steamboat yard and helping Dr. Drake and making his usual observations of the weather and river. It was a life he loved, but he couldn't help but notice that there seemed to be an undercurrent of some sort afoot in Cincinnati. Everywhere he went for Dr. Drake or his father or when he was simply making his scientific observations, there was talk. Talk about the *Philanthropist*, talk about abolition, and most of all, talk about James Birney.

A sunny Saturday afternoon found Henry and Abe finally at the fishing hole on the creek that wound through the edge of Cincinnati on its way to the Ohio River.

"At last we get a day to fish, and they aren't biting," Abe complained.

"It's too hot." Henry rested against a tree at the side of the creek. "The fish are down deep, keeping cool." Absently he scraped at the loose bark on the tree trunk behind him.

"I wish that's where we were, too. Keeping cool, that is." Abe flopped his line to another spot behind a fallen tree that poked its dead limbs slightly out of the water.

"Let's fish a little longer," Henry proposed. "I'd sure like to have some catfish for supper, but if they still aren't biting, we'll go swimming instead."

"Sounds like a good plan."

They fished in silence for a while until Henry asked, "Anything going on with the *Philanthropist* these days?"

"It's been pretty quiet lately. Mr. Birney isn't there much. He usually just brings in the copy when it's ready. Mr. Pugh sets the type, and I do whatever I'm told."

Henry laughed. "Say, do you ever read that paper?" The water rippled slightly when a fish barely broke the surface.

"Most of it. Mr. Pugh lets me take the partly spoiled pages. I read it at night if I'm not too tired."

"My father brings it home most weeks. I've taken to reading it the same as the *Gazette*." Henry moved his line closer to the rippling spot.

"Do you think it's fanatical, like they say?" Abe asked.

Something tugged gently at Henry's line. He pulled it with a jerk only to see his bait fall off. "No. It seems pretty calm to me. Some of the stories about slavery in the South are horrible, but that's just fact."

"Lots of people don't think that it's fact."

"I know, but my father says that those people are acting like those ostriches from Australia that we learned about in a lecture, always hiding their heads in the sand." Henry pulled his line in to the bank. "I've been hearing lots of talk around town, though. Maybe it's nothing, or maybe it will put someone up to something."

"Like what?" Abe asked.

"I don't know, and maybe I don't want to know." Henry jumped up. "These fish aren't biting for nothing. Let's swim." He started unbuttoning his shirt.

"You don't have to convince me," Abe said as he yanked in his pole and began peeling off his clothes as well.

In a few minutes, the most serious issue on Henry's mind was how to duck Abe's head under the cool water of the creek.

CHAPTER 10

Sunday School

"Henry, would you help me deliver the shirts and shifts to Mrs. Jackson tomorrow?" Louisa asked as she looked up from where she was folding shirts and placing them in bundles.

Henry stopped in the door of the dining room, where Louisa was using the big table for folding. "But don't your friends want to go? You've all worked hard."

"I know. I have the sore fingers to prove it." She picked up a big basket sitting on the floor nearby. "Their parents won't let them go. She lives right next to the black section of town. Their parents don't know what to think about a white woman who lives there." Louisa was disappointed for the others but not surprised.

"How about our parents? Are you sure they'll let you go?"

Louisa made a face. "Yes, I can go if you'll go with me. Otherwise I'll have to wait until next week because Mama can't go tomorrow. You'll go, won't you? Please?"

"What's this worth to you, little sister?" Henry teased.

Louisa looked around for something to throw at him, but finding nothing suitable, decided to stand on her dignity. "Of course it's entirely up to you. The delivery can wait until next week if it's not convenient for you."

"Oh, I'll go." Henry gave in. "I'd like to see Mrs. Jackson again. She was interesting and kind of funny."

"Thank you," Louisa said primly but then started giggling and danced around the table. "I can't wait. Can we go early?"

"Early as you want, but it might be a good idea to let Mrs. Jackson get out of bed first."

"I expect you're right, Mr. Smarty." Louisa returned to her folding. "I'll ask Papa at dinner if he would let one of the boys at the yard take a message to her."

So Mrs. Jackson was expecting them the next morning when they arrived at her neat white house on the edge of what most Cincinnati residents called "Little Africa." Her home was a startling contrast to what Louisa could see down the street. Little Africa looked to be a jumble of shacks and flimsy tenement houses built as high as three or four stories.

"This is awful," Louisa whispered to Henry as they

stepped up on Mrs. Jackson's porch.

"I know. I was here last week with Dr. Drake. Another doctor usually covers this part of town nowadays. Dr. Drake had never brought me along when he used to come here. I was too young then he said. I didn't know it was so bad."

Just then the front door flew open, and Mrs. Jackson's stout body filled the doorway. "There you two are. I was so pleased when I got your message. It's such a treat to have visitors. Not many people venture this close to the tenements." She gestured toward the shacks nearby.

"We've brought something for your Sunday school children," Louisa said in a rush. She patted the clothing in the basket over her arm. Henry carried a large basket as well.

"For my children. Why, what on earth?" Mrs. Jackson motioned Henry and Louisa into the front room of her house. "Now what have you sweet youngsters been up to?"

"It was Louisa and her friends," Henry said. "I'm just the delivery boy."

"And I'm not helping ease this delivery," Mrs. Jackson apologized. She quickly rearranged some books and papers on a table to make room for their baskets. "What have you done here, child?"

"It's shirts and shifts for your children. I noticed that you looked at material at the market but said it was too expensive." Louisa put her basket down. "It seems like my friends and I are always sewing some useless bit of fancywork, so we decided to sew shirts and shifts instead."

Mrs. Jackson had peeked into one of the baskets while Louisa talked. Now she held up a child-sized shirt. "This is just wonderful. The children will be so excited. Maybe as

98

excited as I am. There's desperate need in some of the families." She tugged open another package and pulled out two shifts made to fit a couple little girls.

Louisa could see tears shining in the woman's eyes, but her face was wreathed in smiles as she fingered the clothing.

"So nicely made and so many of them. How did you do it, my dear?"

"Our mothers got us started," Louisa said, "and then we just sewed in our spare time." She reached out to touch one of the shirts.

"It must have taken days."

"We were pretty slow at first," Louisa admitted, "but we got faster." She decided not to mention how often discouragement had made her want to quit.

"Goodness, but I'm forgetting my manners," Mrs. Jackson said and carefully refolded the clothing. "Let's sit down and have some tea and cookies. Or perhaps you'd prefer milk with cookies."

"Thank you, ma'am." Louisa smiled her approval. "Milk and cookies would be nice."

In minutes Mrs. Jackson had ushered them into her kitchen, filled with the sweet smell of baking, and sat them down at the table for cookies still warm from the oven. "I've been baking today for Sunday afternoon. I was fortunate enough to come by the fixings for molasses cookies at the market Wednesday."

"Another bargain?" Henry asked as they bit into the cookies.

"Yes, indeed. Usually I'm forced by circumstances to limit my cooking for the children to the staples that sustain life." Mrs. Jackson poured some milk into glasses for all three of them. "My considered opinion is that molasses cookies should be considered a staple of life, but alas, that's not the commonly held view." She chuckled deeply and sat down to eat a cookie with Henry and Louisa.

"They're delicious," Louisa said as she picked up a stray crumb from the table and stuck it in her mouth.

"God has been wonderfully generous this week. He always provides, but the clothing is beyond expectation. I can't thank you enough."

"You're welcome," Louisa said. She felt sorry that the other girls hadn't been able to come along to share in the fun of delivering the results of all their hard work.

"Where do you hold your Sunday school classes?" Henry asked.

"Generally we meet right in there in my front room. They sit on the floor if there aren't enough chairs. My helper Sarah and I often split the group so some of them can sit at this table to practice writing their letters."

"I didn't know you had a helper," Louisa said.

"Oh, yes. Sarah is a jewel. I couldn't manage without her. She lives with me, and when she isn't working at her job, she is usually helping me with something for the Sunday school."

"Is she a schoolteacher during the week?" Henry asked.

"Oh, no. She's a servant." Mrs. Jackson offered more cookies. "In fact, the house where she works isn't far from yours."

The clock in Mrs. Jackson's front room began to chime. "We'd better go," Henry said. "It's ten o'clock already."

Soon they were on the front porch, where Mrs. Jackson was thanking them once again. "You just can't imagine the good that new clothing does for these children. Besides being a vital need met, it helps them believe that they have worth. They lead very difficult lives, and if they are ever to better themselves, they must be convinced that they deserve more. The clothing helps accomplish that almost as much as the schooling or the Bible stories."

"We are glad we could help," Louisa said. It was hard for her to imagine a life where a new shirt could matter so much.

"I have an idea," Mrs. Jackson said, her face lit up with pleasure. "I don't know why I didn't think of this before. Perhaps, if your parents are willing, you and Henry and any of your friends who want to could come to visit our Sunday school this Sunday afternoon. It's a special occasion already with the new shirts and shifts."

"And the cookies," Louisa reminded her.

Mrs. Jackson laughed. "Yes, and the cookies. The children would love to show off their new finery and could be persuaded to recite some Bible verses, too, I'm sure."

Louisa looked at Henry, who gave a slight nod of his head.

"We'd love to come if our parents permit," Louisa said.

So it was settled. Louisa and Henry hurried on home, talking excitedly all the way, hopeful that their parents would allow them to attend on Sunday.

Their parents thought it was a good idea as long as Henry and Louisa didn't go any farther than Mrs. Jackson's house. That condition was easily met, so the only thing left was for Louisa to impatiently wait for Sunday afternoon to arrive.

She invited Martha and the others, but not unexpectedly, they couldn't go.

The church service seemed especially long that morning, but at last it was over, and soon the Lankfords had finished a simple dinner.

"Henry, hurry up," Louisa called up the stairs. "We don't want to be late." She tied on her bonnet and waited by the front door.

"We couldn't possibly take this long to walk to Mrs. Jackson's," Henry said as he came slowly down the stairs.

"You never know. Something might delay us."

Henry just shook his head. "We're going to be way early. Mark my words."

"Now children, be careful." Mama brushed at Henry's shirt and straightened Louisa's bonnet.

"We will, Mama," Louisa said and opened the front door.

"Here, Son." Papa handed Henry some coins. "Give this to Mrs. Jackson. It's an offering for the Sunday school."

Of course Henry was right, and they reached Mrs. Jackson's house well before the appointed time of two o'clock. Nonetheless, there were small black children shyly peeking from behind Mrs. Jackson's skirt when she answered their knock.

"Come in, come in." Her voice boomed a joyful welcome. "I'm so glad that you could come. The children are terribly excited. As you can see, they are plenty early. Hoping to get the first look at you two, I suspect."

Louisa looked down at the children, who eyed her with a solemn regard. Each one was dressed in either a new shirt or one of the simple dresses made by Louisa and her friends.

When she smiled at them, their faces lit up in return.

"I delivered the clothes yesterday," Mrs. Jackson said as she led the way toward the kitchen. "That made it more likely that they would arrive today clean and ready to learn."

Indeed, most of the children looked positively scrubbed, although there were a few exceptions. Louisa thought that, clean or not, they all looked exceedingly thin.

"First we eat at this school." Mrs. Jackson went to the stove and stirred a big pot that was simmering.

"May we help?" Louisa asked.

"You surely may. Why don't you start slicing that bread, Louisa? And Henry, would you get the bowls and spoons out of that cupboard?"

While they worked, more children arrived and peeked into the kitchen at the new helpers. Promptly at two o'clock Mrs. Jackson rang a small bell, and the children gathered in the front room.

"Now children, we will pray. Please bow your heads with me." Obediently they lowered their heads while their teacher prayed. "We thank You, Lord, for the great bounty You have given us this day. We thank You for the food to nourish our bodies and for the learning to nourish our minds. We thank You, too, for sending Louisa and Henry to learn with us. And lastly, we thank You for the fine clothes that Louisa and her friends made and gave to us. Please bless them for their generosity and help us to be worthy of receiving it. We pray this prayer in our Lord's name. Amen."

In a flash the children were scrambling to line up by the kitchen door. Louisa smiled. Evidently they didn't have to be told the routine for eating. She helped dish up the soup while

Henry handed out bread. The children stood around the kitchen table elbow to elbow while they ate. There was little sound other than the scraping of spoons on bowls. It wasn't until they were almost finished that there began to be a little jostling and talk.

"Mrs. Jackson," a voice called from the front of the house, "I'm so sorry I'm late. I couldn't get away any earlier." A young black woman rushed into the kitchen.

"Now, Sarah, don't fret. I was sure you'd just been delayed at work." Mrs. Jackson waved her hand that held a big dipper. "Besides, as you can see, our visitors have pitched in to help." She introduced Louisa and Henry to her helper.

Louisa smiled at the young woman and then looked closer. Sarah seemed very familiar. She could tell by the other woman's expression that she had also recognized Louisa. Then she remembered. Sarah was the woman who had fallen that day when the girls were out walking. The one who had been tripped by the two boys.

"It's nice to see you again, Sarah."

"You two have met?" Mrs. Jackson asked.

"Yes, a few weeks ago," Sarah said and explained. "Louisa was very kind."

"I guess that's a common thing for Louisa," Mrs. Jackson said and smiled. "These children are full and getting rowdy. Let's start classes."

Soon the group was efficiently divided with Mrs. Jackson taking the older ones into the kitchen for reading and writing practice while Sarah gathered the smallest ones around her to tell them Bible stories. Louisa and Henry helped where they could and just listened part of the time.

After awhile the students changed places, and in this way a couple hours passed quickly. The lessons were simple—just the bare basics of reading and writing—but Louisa could see determination in each face.

Finally the children had a performance of sorts as they took turns reciting Bible verses for their guests. From the very smallest child who shyly recited "Jesus wept," to the older boy who proudly reeled off one of the begat sections from the Old Testament, the students stood tall as they proudly showed off their skills.

"They want to be able to read the Bible," Sarah said while she and Louisa were readying the cookies as a final treat. "Their parents can't read well enough to find a Scripture passage, if at all. They don't want their children to be the same way."

"Mrs. Jackson mentioned that once before," Louisa said. "Where is your family, if you don't mind my asking?"

"My parents are gone now," Sarah replied. "We lived in Philadelphia when I was a child. My father was a businessman."

"So you've always been free," Louisa said as she stacked cookies on a platter.

"Oh, yes. My father immigrated from England as a young man." Sarah brushed at the crumbs on the table with her hands. "I'm free, or at least as free as a black woman can ever be."

Louisa saw that Sarah's face was resigned rather than angry. She wondered if she could be the same if she was in Sarah's shoes. In a few minutes the children crowded around to receive cookies. Their faces were bright and hopeful. Louisa vowed never to forget what joy could be brought about by the simple gift of a new shirt and a molasses cookie.

CHAPTER 11
Abe's Story

Early the next Wednesday morning, Henry took some measurements down at the river's edge. The river was muddy looking after rain the day before, and Henry carefully noted that in a small book that he carried in his pocket. He had promised his father that he'd come early to the shipyard because Dr. Drake was once again gone on a teaching trip.

The shipyard was bustling as usual when he got there and

went directly toward the office to write out some invoices.

"Henry, have you heard?" One of the yard boys called from where he was sweeping up sawdust by the big steam-powered saw that was used to cut the long planks for the steamboat decks.

"Heard what?" Henry asked.

"About the ruckus over at that newspaper place." The boy glanced around. "You know, that abolitionist paper."

"The *Philanthropist*?" Henry asked.

"That's the one."

"What happened? What do you mean?" Henry's mind raced through all the possibilities and couldn't settle on anything.

"Jeremiah!" A shout came from the other side of the saw. "Get yourself back to work." It was the foreman in charge.

The boy shrugged and darted back to sweep vigorously.

Henry hurried on to the office to find his father. He would surely know what had happened. Papa was seated at his desk working but looked up when he saw Henry.

"I can tell by your face, Son, that you've heard the story about the paper." He got up and came around his desk.

"I didn't hear much. What happened?"

"I don't know the whole story either, but apparently there was some sort of break-in at the printing shop last night. The printing press was damaged, but that's all I know."

Henry frowned. "What about Abe? Was anyone hurt?" His friend would surely have been in his small room over the print shop.

"I haven't heard that anyone was hurt, but why don't you

run on over there and check on Abe?" Papa put his hand on his son's shoulder. "We can get along without you for that long."

"Thank you." Henry grinned with relief. He didn't relish waiting until dinnertime to check on Abe. Quickly he sprinted out the door and down the street.

The sidewalk in front of the print shop was littered with torn pieces of paper, and several men stood in a group, talking. The front door of the print shop was hanging by one hinge, and there were more men inside. Henry walked up and looked in. Printing type was scattered everywhere among heaps of torn paper. Pieces of what looked like the press itself were also lying about. A quick glance showed Henry that the torn paper was what was left of the latest issue of the *Philanthropist*.

"Henry!"

"Abe!" Henry looked up to see his friend coming from the back room of the shop. "Are you all right? What happened?" Abe looked fine, although his hair hadn't seen a comb, and his shirt was only half tucked into his dark brown pants.

"I'm fine." His face split into a big grin. "We had a little dustup here last night."

"I'd say so. What happened?" Henry asked again. Just then Mr. Pugh came out of the back room. The big man looked like he hadn't slept at all the night before. He went over to one of the men and began to speak quietly to him.

"Let's go outside," Abe said, "and I'll tell you all about it."

The boys went across the street and sat down on a step in some shade. The July sun was already bouncing off the

THE AMERICAN ADVENTURE

buildings, making the street feel like an oven.

"I was asleep," Abe began, "when a noise woke me up. I thought it was some drunkard in the street until I heard the door come off. Then I got scared. I was trying to decide whether to climb out the back window to go for Mr. Pugh when someone rushed up the stairs and grabbed me as quick as you please."

"What did you do?" Henry couldn't keep from shivering in spite of the heat.

"Not much," Abe admitted. "They knew I was there and came directly after me. It was dark, so I couldn't even see any faces. They blindfolded me and told me to sit down and keep quiet." He grinned sheepishly. "I think I was yelling. A lot."

"Anyone would have been," Henry said. "What happened next?"

"They said that they weren't going to hurt me. That they were blindfolding me so I wouldn't be a witness to anything." Abe shrugged his shoulders. "So I sat down and kept quiet and listened."

"Then they tore up the press and the papers?"

Abe nodded. "I could hear them arguing. Some of them wanted to cart the whole press off or smash it. One of them, I think he was the leader, said it was enough to just take the press apart. Said that would get the point across along with tearing up the newspapers."

"What point?" Henry asked.

"It was a warning to Mr. Pugh and even more to Mr. Birney. I guess they were telling them that they better quit printing their abolitionist newspaper here."

"That's terrible," Henry said. He couldn't believe that something like this could happen in Cincinnati. It went against everything he had been taught about how to settle disputes and disagreements. "Did they leave then?"

"After they had made the biggest mess they could, they left. I waited a couple minutes to make sure it was safe, and then I took off my blindfold and ran for Mr. Pugh."

"Did Mr. Birney come?"

Abe nodded. "He's been here all morning along with some of the committee members of the Cincinnati Anti-slavery Society. The society pays for the newspaper, at least until it gets more subscribers."

"What do you think will happen?" Henry asked.

"They've already fixed the press, so I'm sure they'll keep printing. I'd better get back to the shop." Abe stood up and tucked in his shirt.

Henry got up, too. "I better get going, too. I'm glad you're not hurt."

"Thanks." Abe grinned again. "And you said nothing exciting ever happens in Cincinnati."

"Was I ever wrong," Henry said with a laugh. He waved and made his way back toward the shipyard. What a story Abe had to tell. It was exciting, but it was also scary. And it wasn't the fun kind of scary.

There was lots of talk that day and the next, but the citizens of Cincinnati seemed to be waiting to see what would happen next.

Thursday evening Henry burst into the front door of his house. "Look what I found!" He held up the handbill that he

111

had found tacked to a post at the corner of their street.

His father looked up from the newspaper he had been reading. He sat in his big chair in the front room with the evening light from the window illuminating his paper. "What did you find?"

Louisa came skidding down the polished floor of the hallway. "What is it?"

"What's this running and yelling about?" Mama came out of the kitchen and followed her daughter into the front room. "Your manners are sadly lacking."

"Excuse me," Henry said. "I couldn't wait to show this to you." He waved the handbill.

"What is it?" Louisa repeated impatiently.

Papa stood up and took the piece of paper from his son. "Abolitionists beware," he read aloud. Quickly he glanced over the rest of the text. "Why it's a warning against resuming the printing of the *Philanthropist*."

Mama and Louisa crowded close to read over his arm. "If an attempt is made to reestablish their press, it will be viewed as an act of defiance to an already outraged community, and on their own heads be the results which follow," Louisa read.

"The press has already been reestablished," Henry said. "They're working on the next issue." He looked at his father, who was frowning. "What do you think will happen?"

"I don't know," answered Papa. "I'd like to think this is the work of some rabble-rousing misfit, but that's not what it sounds like. This language indicates a well-thought-out threat to the *Philanthropist*. Wrong, but well thought out."

"There could be more trouble?" Mama asked.

"A lot more trouble," her husband replied grimly.

The next few days were quieter than Henry had expected. As he went about his work and errands and observations, he found out about meetings between the Antislavery Society and the mayor and other city leaders. The newspapers printed nasty attacks on the abolitionists. There was talk and more talk, but nothing happened. Finally Henry heard that a public meeting was scheduled for Saturday evening, July 23, at the Market House. Perhaps that would bring the issue to a head and resolve it.

Late Saturday afternoon found Henry and Louisa on an unexpected errand. They were to deliver some soup and other food to Miss Emma. Their mother had just discovered that the elderly woman was not feeling well. Since Mama and Papa were due at a dinner at the home of a business associate, it fell to Henry and Louisa to take the food to Miss Emma and check on her well-being.

"Land's sake, children," Miss Emma said from her wooden rocking chair, "it's just a touch of a summer cold. Your sweet mother needn't have gone to so much trouble." She thanked them several times and promised that she was just fine. In a few minutes they were on their way home.

"We could go home by way of the street by the Market House," Henry said casually. "It's practically on the way."

"Where the meeting is?"

Henry nodded. He could see Louisa's eyes shining with excitement at the suggestion.

"Do we dare?" she asked.

"I don't see why not. It's a public street, and it's a public

113

meeting," Henry said with a shrug.

"Will Mama and Papa care?"

Henry hesitated. "I don't know. They probably wouldn't mind if we just looked at where the meeting was being held. We shouldn't go inside or anything. We won't go if you don't want to." He meant what he said, but he sure hoped his sister would agree.

"Let's go," Louisa said firmly and turned down a side street.

Henry grinned at his sister. He often admired her ability to make a quick decision, right or wrong. She didn't get so wrapped up looking at all the possibilities as he did.

People crowded the sidewalk and spilled into the street in front of the Market House. An occasional squeal revealed that the ever-present pigs were attending, too. Henry and Louisa stationed themselves on a bench in front of a store on the opposite side of the street. They had a good view there of the activity.

"A lot of men are going in," Louisa said.

"I think they set the meeting time so it would catch the foundry and shipyard workers as they came home from their jobs."

"It worked."

At last the street and then the sidewalk cleared as everyone went inside the Market House. Reluctantly Henry stood up. "I guess we should go now."

"Hmm, I was thinking." Louisa looked up at Henry. "Perhaps we should go over there." She pointed across the street. "Not go in. Just stand by one of those windows on the side."

114

"Why would we do that?" Henry asked with lifted eyebrows. His little sister was trying to look innocent.

"So we can be well informed? Or something like that. Please, Henry. This is our chance to be the first to know what's going on."

Henry looked across the street and then back at Louisa. This was one of those times that being the oldest was hard. "Oh, all right, but just for a few minutes."

"Thanks," Louisa said. She grabbed him by the arm and started across the street, dodging the lone pig that still snuffled in the gutter.

They positioned themselves under one of the big open windows that were above head level even for Henry. From there they could hear what was being said inside. At first Henry felt like they were eavesdropping, even though it was a public meeting. In a few minutes he was so caught up in the proceedings that he forgot where he was.

The meeting hadn't actually started yet. He could hear the rumble of conversation with an occasional recognizable phrase floating out. Then there was shouting and someone hammered something—probably a gavel. Gradually the audience grew quiet. By listening carefully, Henry could understand almost everything being said at the front of the room.

Louisa disappeared briefly around the side of the building next door and returned triumphantly, carrying a somewhat rickety-looking stool, evidently salvaged from the waste pile out behind the building. She daintily dusted the stool with her hand and sat down. Henry just shook his head at her resourcefulness.

The meeting participants inside were opening with prayer. Henry was only too happy to join them in praying for a peaceful solution to this prickly problem.

A man Henry knew to be the postmaster seemed to be in charge and spoke first. Mr. Burke said, "Our purpose for this meeting is to decide whether the citizens of Cincinnati will permit the publication or distribution of abolition newspapers in this city."

Immediately after Mr. Burke came another man who spoke of slavery as a great evil but not one that could be fixed by the present generation. Several speakers said much the same thing, and each one was applauded at great length.

"Much as we deplore this institution of slavery, we value our kinship with our southern neighbors more," said another man who was called Judge by Mr. Burke. "Our close ties with our neighbors compel us to put a stop to the madness that is incited by the content of these abolitionist papers. What offends them, offends us."

Louisa stood up and pulled Henry's head down so she could talk in his ear. "He's talking money, isn't he?"

Henry nodded slowly. Louisa was quick to pick up on what Henry had been thinking all week. The businessmen in Cincinnati were afraid of losing business with the southern states like Kentucky a lot more than they were worried about anything directly related to slavery.

The crowd inside became more vocal in their support of restricting the abolitionists. Henry heard only one gentleman speak about free speech, but even he used that to warn the abolitionists not to preach sectional hatred.

"This paper must be put down," a man declared, "peaceably if possible, forcibly if not."

In the pause that greeted this harsh statement, Henry heard a loud clatter beside him. Unconsciously he had turned away from Louisa as he strained to hear the speakers. Now he jerked around to see that his sister was holding onto the window ledge with her hands while her feet dangled freely. The broken stool lay in a heap to one side.

"What are you doing?" he hissed and grabbed her around the middle before she could fall.

"I was just trying to see. I thought the stool would hold me."

"Girl, what are you doing out here eavesdropping?" a deep voice demanded from the open window above. Henry looked up to see that the window framed a bear of a man. Huge and hairy, the man looked downright mean as he scowled down at them. Time to beat a retreat.

"Come on," Henry said and grabbed Louisa's arm. "We were just leaving," he said to the man.

Louisa pulled away. "It's a public meeting." She crossed her arms and gave the man a cold stare. "I can listen if I want."

"Is that so, missy?" Suddenly a leg was thrown over the windowsill. "We'll just see about that," came his muffled voice.

"Maybe we will be going after all," Louisa said and took off running. Henry was right behind her. They didn't stop until they were a block away.

"You about got us knocked in the head," Henry accused.

"It was pretty exciting, wasn't it?" Louisa was windblown but wore a satisfied smile.

Henry rolled his eyes. The last few days had held more excitement than he could handle. After this meeting, he didn't know what to expect next.

CHAPTER 12
In the River

Henry found out later that the meeting at the Market House produced a committee of twelve men who were to meet with James Birney and the Antislavery Society leaders. They were instructed to warn the abolitionists that if they persisted in publishing their paper, the committee could not be held responsible for the consequences.

Henry was thinking about that ultimatum the following Saturday afternoon when he worked late at the shipyard, where they were shorthanded in the office because of illness. It didn't help that his father had gone to Pittsburgh to check on some engine parts that had been delayed in shipment.

Henry sat at a desk, copying invoices, but the going was slow. He couldn't keep from thinking about all that had happened.

"Did you see this?" One of the clerks stopped beside the table where Henry was working. He held out a newspaper and pointed to a notice printed on the front page. The headline read "Antislavery Society Defiant." The short article reported the failure of the Market House committee to convince the society to cease publication of the *Philanthropist*. A public meeting was scheduled for six o'clock Saturday evening to chart a course of action. Henry looked up at the clock on a nearby shelf. Almost six o'clock now.

"Thanks," he said and hastily stacked the invoices. The meeting was at the Exchange Hotel, which wasn't far away. This time he was going in and at least stand in the back. No listening under windows.

The meeting was underway when he slipped into the back of the room. At first he thought he must be in the wrong place because the participants were calmly electing a chairman and secretary. They then proceeded to pass a series of resolutions that called for the destruction of the abolitionist press and the tarring and feathering of James Birney. There was agreement among them to meet after dark at the corner of Main and Seventh to get on with the work to be done.

Henry didn't wait to hear anything else. He swung out the door and started toward the print shop. He had to warn Abe and Mr. Pugh.

The print shop door was locked, already closed for the day. He ran around to the side of the building where the outside stairs were and quickly climbed to the landing. Abe's room opened onto the landing. He knocked on the door, but there was no answer. Abe must be at Mr. Pugh's house, where he ate his meals. But Henry didn't know which house that was. He stood on the landing for a moment unsure what to do next. He needed to warn someone, but who?

"Henry!"

It was Abe, yelling from the alley below the stairs. Henry pounded down the steps. He said a quick prayer of thanks. Quickly he explained to his friend what he had seen and heard at the Exchange Hotel. Abe's face grew serious.

"We better go warn Mr. Pugh," Henry said. "Maybe he can get the city watch to come."

"He's not at home," Abe replied slowly. "The Pughs left this afternoon to visit some of his wife's family. They'll be back late tonight."

"What about Mr. Birney? Let's get him."

Abe shook his head. "He's gone, too. He went to Lebanon to give a lecture. I heard him telling Mr. Pugh."

"I wish my father was home. He'd know what to do." Henry glanced at the sky. "It'll be dark soon, and that's when they're meeting. Let's go to my house and talk to my mother."

"Mama went to Miss Emma's," Louisa told the two boys when they burst in through the front door a few minutes later. "Miss Emma is feeling worse."

"What do we do now?" Abe asked.

"What's wrong? What are you talking about?" Louisa asked. "Why have you been running? Do you want a drink of water?" She led the way back to the kitchen.

"There's a mob getting ready to destroy Mr. Pugh's printing press and tar and feather Mr. Birney," Henry said.

He ran his hands through his hair. What now? Where could they go for help?

"Oh, no!" Louisa said in a small voice. Her face turned pale in the fading evening light. "We have to do something. Those horrible men." She handed Abe the water dipper.

Henry frowned as he thought. "We should go back to the print shop. Maybe we can get the watch to help stop them."

"Maybe," Abe said, "but Mr. Birney said he thought the watch just stood by when the shop was broken into the first time."

"We have to try." He grabbed the dipper for a quick sip of water. "Let's go." His voice was determined. There must be some way to stop this madness.

"I'll go with you," Louisa said.

"No!" Henry said more loudly than he intended. "You stay here and tell Mama when she gets back. Maybe she can send someone to help. Where's Anna anyhow?"

"Her brother came to fetch her right after Mama left," Louisa said. "His wife was about to have a baby. I told her to go ahead. I'd be fine here alone until you got home."

"I'm sorry to leave you here, but it's too dangerous for you to go along." Henry knew that Louisa would be angry to be left behind, but he just couldn't risk taking her into the unknown—not when he'd seen how much damage an uncontrolled mob could do.

Louisa's eyes sparked for a moment, but then her brother saw her take a deep breath. "All right, I'll stay here, but be careful and come back as soon as you can."

"Thanks." Henry grinned at his little sister, who suddenly seemed a lot more grown up.

It was almost dark when Henry and Abe reached the appointed corner. They concealed themselves in a nearby doorway to watch. At first it was just a crowd of men who gathered there. But within minutes that crowd became a mob, noisily intent on destroying property and threatening life. The transformation momentarily mesmerized Henry.

"We better see if we can find the watch," Abe said urgently.

The boys kept to the shadows and moved away from the surging mob, which was headed down the middle of the street. A few held torches, and a couple men carried lanterns. In no time, Henry spotted a member of the night watch standing near a building no more than half a block from the mob. He seemed to be observing the goings-on but making no move to do anything.

Henry raced up to the man. "You've got to do something," he said. "They're going to destroy the press. They're talking about tarring and feathering James Birney."

"Now, son, just calm down." The tall man stood up a little straighter. "I reckon what's happening is meant to be. You might even say that it's God's will. Now we wouldn't want to be messing around with what's God's will, would we?" The man was almost genial.

"I can't see that it could be God's will that property be destroyed by a mob. Someone might get hurt." Henry couldn't believe what he was hearing. He looked at Abe, who raised his eyebrows and shook his head. "So you're not going to do anything?"

"I've got my orders. Now you two run on home before you get in the way." The watchman shooed the boys in the opposite direction from the mob.

They obeyed until they reached a side street. Without speaking, they circled back at a dead run until they were ahead of the mob, which by that time had almost reached the print shop.

Gasping for breath after the run, the boys hid in a recessed doorway across the street. "What can we do?" Abe asked when he had caught his breath.

"I don't know." Henry stared at the mob that sprawled over the street like a mindless blob. "I don't think we can do anything. At least not by ourselves. If the watch is in on it, who else is there?"

So they watched as the mob rushed the print shop door and quickly broke it open. In moments a hail of books, type, pieces of the press, and other office equipment was hurled out the windows. A crowd of spectators soon gathered to watch as the whole print shop was torn apart. Then there was a lull, when nothing seemed to be happening. Was it over?

"Are they done?" Abe echoed his friend's thoughts.

"Maybe," Henry said. He strained his eyes through the darkness, but there was nothing to see.

Suddenly the press itself appeared in the doorway. In seconds the mob shoved it through the door with a tremendous heave. Cheers broke out among the spectators. Henry's heart sank. What now?

There was scrambling as several men attached ropes to the heavy press. In a few minutes they dragged it triumphantly down the street. Onlookers scattered to get out of the way.

"To the river!" someone shouted.

"They're going to dump it in the Ohio," Henry said incredulously. He pulled at Abe's arm, and they ran along behind the spectators, who yelled out encouragement to the men dragging the press.

It didn't take long to get to the riverfront, but the mob spent long minutes positioning the press so it could be shoved into the river without taking anyone along. Henry and Abe ventured close enough so that Henry could see some of the faces in the mob. They seemed ordinary enough but for the wild look in their eyes.

"Isn't that the mayor over there?" Abe asked as he jabbed Henry in the ribs and pointed to a nearby group of onlookers.

Henry peered through the flickering light of lanterns and torches. "I think you're right. What's he doing here? Why doesn't he do something?"

Abe just shook his head slowly and didn't say a word.

Anger built in Henry as he looked at Mayor Davies. Why didn't he call the watch to stop this mob? How could he stand there silently watching as the press was destroyed?

Henry had no answers for his own questions. Then came a splash followed by cheers. Henry darted forward on the dock to see the Ohio River waters closing around the press as it quickly sank out of sight. Too late now.

But it seemed the mob wasn't finished yet. No sooner was the press out of sight when someone shouted, "Birney! Let's get Birney."

"Get the tar and feathers!" The mob milled around momentarily and then surged back down the street away from the river.

Henry and Abe fell back to watch. "At least we know that Mr. Birney isn't home," Henry said. He hoped the mob would be mightily disappointed to find the target of their anger out of reach.

"Shall we follow them?" Abe asked.

"Let's go back to my house first," Henry replied. "If my mother is there, she'll be worried about us. And Louisa might be there all alone. Surely the mob will go home once they don't find Mr. Birney." Even as he made that statement, he heard someone yelling about going down to Church Alley and stirring things up. He knew that Church Alley was in Little Africa. Everything was falling apart, and nothing he could say was going to help. For now he just wanted to get home.

Louisa was still home alone. Her mother hadn't returned yet. Louisa had seldom been in the house by herself and never at night, but she assured herself several times that she was perfectly able to take care of herself. That helped her feel a little better, but she also lit every lamp she could find. Finally she settled at the kitchen table and ate bread with apple butter. Where was Henry? When she'd stuck her head out the front door a few minutes earlier, she thought she could hear shouting. The *Philanthropist* office was a good distance from their house, but perhaps the sounds would carry in the night air.

She longed for her father to walk in the door but knew that he couldn't possibly return for another day. Then there was a noise at the door. The hair on the back of her neck prickled. Maybe she was just a little nervous. After all, this wasn't any ordinary Saturday evening. She peeked out of the kitchen down the hallway. The breath she had been holding gushed out when she saw that it was Henry and Abe coming in the front door.

"What happened? Did they destroy the press? Was there a fight?" Her questions tumbled out.

"Mama isn't back yet?" Henry asked, ignoring her questions.

"No, I'm afraid that Miss Emma must be worse than we thought. Please just tell me what happened." She didn't like the grim expression on her brother's face.

Henry paced in the hallway for a few moments and then went back outside on the front porch to look down the street. At last he turned toward Louisa, who had followed him, along with Abe, and began to recount the last hour's events.

The apple butter and bread churned in Louisa's stomach a little as she listened to the story. It was worse than she had expected. How could the mayor just stand by and let those awful men dump the press in the river? And what did they mean about stirring up things in the black section of town? When Henry finished his tale, she walked over to stare through the darkness to the west, wishing she could see what was happening in Little Africa. Henry and Abe stood talking quietly to each other, but she had heard enough.

Thoughts ran through her head in a jumble, and at first she didn't identify the faint orange glow in the distance. As if waking up, she suddenly realized that it was a fire. "Look!" she yelled. The boys jerked around and looked where Louisa pointed.

"They've set a fire," Henry said. "It could be in Little Africa from the looks of it." He rubbed his forehead briefly. "Where will it end?"

Louisa stared at her brother in horror. "Do something, Henry! Don't let them burn up the houses." She grabbed his arm.

"I don't think there's anything I can do." His voice was quiet, and he put his hand on Louisa's shoulder. "The people who could stop it won't."

"But the mob is in Little Africa," she said. "What about Mrs. Jackson and the children and Sarah?"

"The children will be in their homes," he replied quickly. "Their parents will take care of them."

"But Mrs. Jackson? Some people don't like it that she helps the black people. What about her and Sarah? Who will help them?"

Henry stared at her. His deep frown made him look years older to Louisa as she stared back. "We've got to help them." Her voice was low and urgent.

Henry took a deep breath and looked at Abe, who nodded slightly. "All right. Abe and I will go bring them back here."

"I'm coming, too," Louisa said flatly. "You don't need to argue. I'm not staying here alone any longer. We'll stick to the back streets. They're my friends, too." She gave Henry a defiant look but was afraid that he wouldn't agree. She used her last threat. "I'll go by myself if you don't let me go with you." She wasn't exactly sure that she'd act on her threat, but Henry didn't know that.

Henry flashed her a look that would have melted butter

on a cold day. "Louisa! You're impossible." He turned to Abe. "Come on. We might as well take her now as after the argument." He looked at his sister. "If it gets dangerous, you have to promise to do what I say, even if that's to come home."

"I promise. What are we waiting for? Let's go." She started down the sidewalk.

"Wait a minute," her brother ordered. "Put out all those lamps except for one turned low in the entryway. We're likely to have a fire of our own if you don't."

"Right, and we better leave Mama a note in case she gets back." Louisa hoped that didn't happen until they were safely back with Mrs. Jackson and Sarah. Her mother would just worry.

The streets were quiet as they ran from one to another. Quiet until they were almost to Mrs. Jackson's house. The fires had died down, but the sounds of destruction were audible in the distance. Louisa thought the mob must be pulling the shanties apart board by board from the sounds of it.

Mrs. Jackson's house appeared unharmed when it came in sight. Louisa breathed a sigh of relief. But her relief was short-lived. Suddenly flames flared down the street from Mrs. Jackson's tidy house. The mob streamed around the corner at the end of the block, shouting and waving their torches and throwing rocks.

Louisa stood paralyzed by the sight until her brother grabbed her arm and yanked her toward the alley behind Mrs. Jackson's house. "Come on! We don't have any time to spare."

Louisa stumbled but righted herself and hurried after Henry, who still held her arm. *Please God,* she prayed silently. *Let it not be too late to help Mrs. Jackson and Sarah.*

Enough for One Night

Louisa could hear some of the sentences the mob was shouting in front of Mrs. Jackson's house. "Stop here!"someone cried. "She's a slave lover."

Rocks pelted the front porch with a clatter. Louisa and Henry and Abe ran quickly up to Mrs. Jackson's back door, which opened onto the alley.

Henry knocked on the door. Louisa stood back and prayed that the woman would hear the knock and the mob in front would not. At last Louisa pushed up to the door and called urgently to her friend. "Mrs. Jackson! Please open up. It's Louisa Lankford."

"Louisa, child. Is that you?" An astonished Mrs. Jackson threw the bolt on the door, and the three children slipped into her kitchen. "What on earth? You children shouldn't be here."

"We've come to get you," Louisa said. "It's too danger-ous here."

"Land's sake, girl. Don't I just know it." Mrs. Jackson managed a chuckle.

A window suddenly shattered with a crash, and the mob could be heard more clearly.

"Where's Sarah?" Henry asked.

"She's in the hallway with our weapons," Mrs. Jackson replied and called to the young woman. Sarah appeared in the kitchen door armed with a fireplace poker in one hand and a rolling pin in the other. Her face was tight with fear.

Another crash made them all jump. "We've got to go," Henry said. "Quick, out the back!"

Louisa took Sarah's arm and pulled her out the back door. The others followed.

They hurried silently down the alley. Behind them the mob was still milling around in front of the house, yelling and throwing the occasional rock. Louisa glanced behind them, and what she saw made her breath catch in her throat. Some of the men had gone around to the side of the house and were peering down the alley.

Before she could say anything, a shout announced what she had seen to the others.

"Uh, oh," Henry said. "They've seen us. Faster, we've got to move faster." Without discussion, he moved to one side of Mrs. Jackson, and Abe moved to the other. Together they helped her navigate at top speed down the dark alley. Louisa and Sarah were right behind them.

At the corner they turned right back onto the street. They could hear someone behind them curse as he tripped over some garbage. Those few seconds gave Henry time to guide the group down another alley. By this time Mrs. Jackson was puffing from running so hard. Henry said something to Abe and then turned back to Louisa and Sarah. "We've got to hide. We can't run any farther."

Henry ran ahead, checking the doors of the businesses that opened onto this alley. At last he found what he was looking for—an unlocked back door that led into a storeroom. He motioned for them to go in the door.

"Should we be going in here?" Louisa asked. It didn't seem right to just open a door and walk in.

"We don't have any choice," Henry said and shoved his sister over the threshold. They all crouched there and waited and listened. In a few seconds there was the sound of pounding feet in the alley and loud discussion about the prey that was getting away. But the door stayed safely shut, and the men's voices faded in the distance. Louisa breathed again, thankful to have escaped.

Her relief was interrupted when a lamp flared in the inside doorway leading to the front of the building.

"What have we here?" a man's voice said. Louisa looked through the dim light and saw an older man with an apron tied around his waist. He held the lamp high as he surveyed the five uninvited guests still crouched on the storeroom floor.

"The mob was after us," Henry said, "and your door was unlocked." He stood up and introduced himself and the others.

Mrs. Jackson struggled to rise up from her cramped position. "Sir, we certainly understand that you might be a bit upset at our coming in like this. It seemed the prudent thing to do when those idiots out there were breathing down our necks."

The man just looked at them for a few moments. Louisa watched him tensely. One shout from him, and the mob would be on them.

At last she heard a rumble of laughter. "You've got one thing right. Those men out there are idiots." He set his lamp down on a nearby crate. "The day men take the law into their own hands is a day of doom for free men everywhere. They've lost sight of the freedoms some of our fathers and grandfathers fought for." He shook his head, his face now sober. "Well, what's done is done. Let's see what we can do to get you safely out of this neighborhood."

"Thank you," Mrs. Jackson said. "We'd be obliged."

"Try to make yourselves comfortable back here for a little while," the man said. "I'll go out and see what I can see."

So they settled down to wait, sitting on boxes and buckets that were in the storeroom. They chatted some but mostly just sat and waited. Louisa realized how tired she was and how much she wished she were back in her safe home. But was it safe? Would the mob go totally berserk and take their lawless actions throughout the city? She could only pray that God would stay their hands and knock some sense into their heads.

In about an hour the shopkeeper appeared in the door of the storeroom again. "Well, I've good news. The mob has disbanded. I think it's safe for you to venture out."

"What happened?" Louisa asked.

"Did the watch finally stop them?" Henry questioned.

"Actually it was Mayor Davies," the shopkeeper said.

"We saw him watching earlier, and he wasn't doing anything at all," Abe said.

"I know, son. He's one of those idiots we were talking about." The shopkeeper took Mrs. Jackson's hand and helped her up from her seat on a bucket. "But I guess he grew concerned for his lost sleep. He was talking to the crowd when I arrived. He advised them that they had done enough for one night. That surely the abolitionists could see what the public sentiment was. Besides, they were missing out on much needed rest." The shopkeeper shook his head. "So with that eloquent plea for civil order, the mob went home to their neglected beds."

"So I guess that means we can go home, too," Henry said.

"I'd say so," the shopkeeper agreed.

"I think Mrs. Jackson and Sarah should still go home with us," Louisa said. "It can't hurt anything."

"On that subject I'm inclined to agree," Mrs. Jackson said. "I'm not quite ready to go back to that house in the dark."

"I'll walk with you then," the shopkeeper said. "Just in case."

But the streets were quiet once again. Apparently the mayor's reminder of the need for adequate rest had steered the rioters home to bed. The only evidence of the riot was the smell of smoke that hung in the night air.

"What in the world?" Mama's voice startled the group. She was just coming down the sidewalk toward home from the opposite direction. "Mrs. Jackson, are you all right?" Mama hurried to take the older woman's arm.

"Well now, I'm bound to say that I'm just about all in."

Mrs. Jackson shook her head. "But I'm fine, and that's thanks to your children and their friend." Her laugh rolled over them. "You should have seen them flying me through the streets. This big old body of mine hasn't moved so fast in many a year." Her face sobered. "If the children hadn't come after us, I don't know what might have happened."

"I had no idea that things were in such a state," Mama said after hearing what had happened. "I was at Miss Emma's for several hours."

"How is she?" Louisa asked. In all the turmoil, she had forgotten that their old friend was ill.

"She's some better. One of her neighbors came over to sit with her so I could come home. I guess things were under control here, in a manner of speaking," Mama said with a smile. "I'll be happy to hear more about all this later, but for now, let's get some tea brewing and start thinking about beds for everyone. You must be exhausted."

Louisa took Sarah's arm and together they walked back to the kitchen. Louisa could tell by the look on her mother's face that she and Henry would be hearing more about the rescue later. Hopefully the good accomplished would weigh heavily in their favor.

There didn't end up being much time to think about that, however, because the trouble wasn't over yet. Sunday was spent as usual, in church and at home, but there was an uneasiness in the air. By the time Papa arrived home from his trip Sunday evening, Henry had heard that the mob was meeting again. They were determined to find James Birney.

"I can't say that I'm really too surprised at this turn of events," Papa said after they told him what had happened.

He sat down in his chair in the front room. "But I am certainly disappointed that our city leaders wouldn't put a stop to these shenanigans. Why, this is nothing less than mob rule. Please, let's pray that this will end soon." Papa knelt on the polished floor right beside his chair, and the others joined him. They took turns praying that the rioting would cease with no more violence.

But it seemed that there was to be no immediate end to the riots. Sunday night was once again filled with the distant sounds of shouting and breaking glass, but this time the Lankford family and their guests were safely in their home. Henry found it impossible to sleep even after the sounds had faded. He kept thinking of the black children he had met so recently. He tossed on the pallet where he slept beside Abe so Mrs. Jackson could have his bed. What about Mr. Birney? Would someone tell him in time not to show himself when he arrived home from his trip?

Monday morning dawned on a town that seemed to be going about its business. When Abe went off to find Mr. Pugh, Henry went with him. Henry was glad to be allowed to get out of his house and hoped that life could get back to normal.

The print shop looked anything but normal. This time there had been no immediate attempt to clean up the mess. It looked as it had Saturday night after the riot, only now the light of day emphasized the destruction inflicted by the mob. Torn and crumpled bits of newspaper fluttered in the breeze. Type and parts of the press still lay scattered in the street. Someone had righted the broken door, but it still leaned crookedly against the door frame. There was no sign of

Achilles Pugh, but as usual people were standing around talking. Abe ran off to the back to see if he could find Mr. Pugh, while Henry waited and listened.

"This carnival has gone too far," one well-dressed man said. "The next thing you know, that mob will be knocking at all our doors."

Murmurs of assent could be heard in the group gathered near the print shop. A louder voice made Henry turn and look across the street. It was Charles Hammond, the publisher of the *Cincinnati Gazette*.

"I'm pleased to see that you have a respect for authority, sir," Mr. Hammond said, "even though it seems to hinge to a considerable degree on self-interest." He crossed the street to stand beside the group.

"Hammond, you're probably one of those fanatics yourself," someone yelled.

"I assure you that I am not one of those 'fanatics' as you so kindly label the abolitionists," Mr. Hammond replied. Henry edged up closer so he wouldn't miss a word.

Mr. Hammond continued, "In fact, I consider that the abolitionists, being in the minority, ought to have deferred to the obvious wishes of the many, even if that group was totally unenlightened."

Henry looked around to see if the men understood that Mr. Hammond was referring to them as unenlightened. By their nods of approval at the publisher's words, he supposed not.

"Even so," Mr. Hammond continued, "this was no reason why a speck of mischief should be done through nothing more than mob violence."

Members of the group all talked at once. Some quite obviously thought Mr. Hammond had gone too far. Others were nodding their heads reluctantly. At last the man Henry had heard first spoke again.

"We've got to do something. Whatever we think about the abolitionists and slavery and that paper isn't the point. We've got to keep this town from going up in flames."

There was muttering but then silence as the men recognized that they did agree about one thing. Cincinnati had to be saved. Henry watched their faces as they struggled to focus on that one goal.

"How about a citizens' patrol tonight?" someone said. "We'll put a stop to all this foolishness."

And it was in that moment, Henry later thought, that the crisis began to end. He listened as the men organized to patrol the streets that night, and soon he left with Abe to take the news to his father at the shipyard. That night any attempts at raising the mob again were quickly stopped by the patrols.

So the mob vanished, leaving behind no more than some burned-out shanties and a bad taste for the people of Cincinnati. Or at least that was how it seemed to Henry.

In a day or two, he escorted Mrs. Jackson and Sarah back to their home. He helped them fix their broken windows and clean up glass and other debris, but he couldn't shake a sad feeling. How could mere words in a newspaper or spoken aloud have caused this? The worst part for Henry was that everyone still blamed the abolitionists and James Birney for the riot, even though the men hadn't been in the city at the time.

On Thursday of that week, Henry took Louisa with him

to the shipyard to see a brand new steamboat that their father and the workers were launching. It was a grand sight to see the boat slip from the ways into the water with a plop and corresponding splash. It made the events of the last week fade. Life went on.

"Well, if it isn't my abolitionist friend."

Henry turned around from watching the steamboat to see Walter standing on a nearby dock. His sister, Julia, was beside him, and they were dressed for traveling.

"Hi, Walter, Julia. Going somewhere?" Henry asked politely, ignoring the low groan that came from Louisa when she saw the pair. He walked over to stand beside Walter.

"Hello, Julia," Louisa said. "Surely you're not leaving Cincinnati so soon."

"We most certainly are," Julia snapped with only a hint of her accent. "Our papa would not want us here with all of this terrible lawlessness going on."

"You abolitionists have ruined Cincinnati," Walter pronounced.

"I don't recall labeling myself an abolitionist," Henry said.

"Everyone has to be something," Walter said, "and you act like an abolitionist."

There was a certain logic to Walter's statement, Henry had to admit. He had always considered himself to be neutral on many issues. He liked to look carefully at both sides and remain open-minded about the rightness or wrongness of a stand. But sometimes a person just had to get off the fence, he realized.

"You know, Walter," Henry said, "I have to thank you.

You've made it so much easier for me to figure everything out."

Walter looked doubtful. "You're welcome, I think."

Henry laughed and clapped Walter on the back. Maybe the Georgia boy might figure things out himself someday, but it wasn't going to be this day.

The Garnetts went off to board their steamboat bound for Pittsburgh. Henry and Louisa waved goodbye before starting for home.

"Have you had enough excitement this week, little sister? I know how deprived you sometimes feel, being a girl and all."

"Very funny," Louisa said. "I guess I can safely say that I've had my fill of excitement for a day or two."

"Good, because I've been thinking that it's time for you to get started on some wax fruit and velvet painting. Maybe you could even make wax fruit and then paint it on velvet." Henry ducked because Louisa's bonnet came sailing through the air and smacked him in the side of the head. He just laughed and took off running, chased by a somewhat unladylike little sister.

Good News for Readers

There's more! The American Adventure continues with *Fight for Freedom*. Meg and Fred Allerton just can't seem to get along. Fred is always teasing his older sister and getting her into trouble for daydreaming and sketching. For her part, Meg wishes Fred wouldn't be so quick to get into fights and say what he thinks.

They can't even agree on how to solve the problem of slavery. Fred is excited when William Lloyd Garrison opens a store in Cincinnati that won't sell anything produced by slave labor. Meg thinks there must be a way to deal with the issue that won't make people so angry.

Then Meg gets terribly sick. Will Fred come to value the things that make his sister so different from him? And will Meg ever learn to stand up for herself and others?